"I'm going to open the door and we're both going down the manhole," her new bodyguard told her.

"No!" Princess Isabelle attempted to free herself. Her royal motorcade was under attack, but that didn't mean she was going underground.

Levi had her clamped against him so securely she couldn't move more than an inch in any direction. She felt his neatly-trimmed beard brush her temple as he spoke briskly into her ear. "Once I open the door we'll be vulnerable. We need to get below ground as quickly as possible."

Isabelle took a shaky breath. To his credit, though he held her immobile, Levi wasn't squeezing her too hard for her to breathe. Maybe it was that small allowance that made her decide to trust him.

Or maybe it was because she didn't have any choice.

Another blast rocked the air, and the hood from another vehicle crashed against the limousine's windshield.

"We won't be safe if we stay here. We've got to move now."

Books by Rachelle McCalla

Love Inspired Suspense

Survival Instinct
Troubled Waters
Out on a Limb
Danger on Her Doorstep
Dead Reckoning
*Princess in Peril

*Reclaiming the Crown

RACHELLE McCALLA

is a mild-mannered housewife, and the toughest she ever has to get is when she's trying to keep her four kids quiet in church. Though she often gets in over her head, as her characters do, and has to find a way out, her adventures have more to do with sorting out the carpool and providing food for the potluck. She's never been arrested, gotten in a fistfight or been shot at. And she'd like to keep it that way! For recipes, fun background notes on the places and characters in this book and more information on forthcoming titles, visit www.rachellemccalla.com.

PRINCESS IN PERIL

RACHELLE MCCALLA

Love Inspired

™ LOVE INSPIRED BOOKS

ISBN-13: 978-0-373-44462-5

PRINCESS IN PERIL

Copyright © 2011 by Rachelle McCalla

www.LoveInspiredBooks.com

Printed in U.S.A.

The Lord says: Although I sent them far away among the nations and scattered them among the countries, yet for a little while I have been a sanctuary for them in the countries where they have gone. I will gather you from the nations and bring you back from the countries where you have been scattered, and I will give you back the land again.
—*Ezekiel* 11:16–17

To Genevieve the Brave, my princess

Acknowledgments

With thanks and gratitude to my husband Ray,
patient first reader, whose grammar and
spelling skills far exceed my own.

Thanks also to Emily Rodmell, visionary editor,
and all the helpful readers whose insights and
encouragement have helped to hone this story.
I hope you will not be disappointed.

And eternal praise and thanks
to our Lord Jesus Christ, hero of that great epic,
King of Kings and Lord of Lords, Amen.

ONE

The royal motorcade lurched to an unexpected stop. Her Royal Highness Princess Isabelle of Lydia glanced at Levi Grenaldo, her recently appointed bodyguard, expecting him to make some reassuring gesture that would indicate nothing was amiss.

He didn't look her way. In the silvery sheen of his mirrored sunglasses, Isabelle saw only the rear bumper of her brother's limousine sitting still on the road in front of them. The seconds ticked by and they sat, unmoving, in the narrow streets of Sardis, Lydia's capital city.

Something had to be wrong. The motorcade represented the power and pageantry of the royal family and therefore *never* stopped until it arrived at its destination.

"Why are we stopped?"

Levi didn't acknowledge her question, but instead pressed the button for the intercom and told the driver, "Get us off this street."

When the driver hesitated, Levi pressed the button again. "Now."

Much as she wanted to remain calm, Isabelle felt her fingers tighten as they gripped the edge of the leather seat. She didn't like anything about this situation. For one thing, she didn't trust Levi.

He'd been abruptly appointed as her personal bodyguard five days earlier with no explanation given, and on top of that, he didn't fit the profile for a bodyguard. Although he was plenty tall and his shoulders were broad with muscles, he was otherwise trim, and the dark angles of his beard gave his face a scholarly look. Unlike all the bodyguards she'd ever had before, his neck wasn't thicker than his head, and he looked unusually sharp in the tuxedo he wore for the state dinner they were about to attend.

Besides that, the bodyguard read books. Intelligent ones. She'd seen him with his nose buried in political tomes whenever he waited for her to finish an appointment.

Out of place as those attributes seemed, what really bothered her was the way he overrode her requests and limited her freedom. As the eldest daughter of King Philip and Queen Elaine, Isabelle was used to having to change her plans to protect her safety, but Levi's impediments went far beyond the usual. They'd butted heads several times. After three days she'd asked to have him removed, but her father had refused her request.

All her instincts told her something was amiss.

The driver had the car two points into what promised to be an eighteen-point turn on the narrow street when suddenly a deafening blast rent the air, rattling the official limo, and an orange ball of fire seared the sky in front of them.

Levi's hand mashed the intercom button.

"Back! Back! Now!"

A second explosion rocked the air even closer behind them, and Isabelle felt the car shudder. Though the royal limousines were made of bulletproof materials, she doubted they'd be any match for that kind of explosion. Her heart twisted with concern for the rest of her family. Alexander, her only living brother, rode in the limousine ahead of her, which didn't appear to have been damaged by the blast, but her brother and back to the crazy-sounding plan to leap through the manhole. "One, two—"

With no time to protest, Isabelle pinched her eyes shut as Levi opened the door and, in one swift movement, pulled her from the vehicle and shuttled her through the hole in the pavement. Much as she didn't trust him, she knew the danger outside was real, and she didn't want to be exposed to it any longer than was absolutely necessary. For that reason only, she cooperated with his actions.

She opened her eyes as the soles of her leather pumps slid against the slippery metal bars that formed a ladder secured to the wall of the tunnel. Although she couldn't get purchase on any of the rungs, Levi seemed to have a steady hold on both the ladder and her. She wished she'd chosen to wear something a bit more practical than a silk, floor-length evening gown, but the dress had been the perfect choice for the state dinner she was now about to miss.

Her trembling hands reached for the bars, and she managed to grip one securely.

"Hold on tight." Levi's instructions sounded close to her ear. "Got it?"

Unable to muster up words, she nodded. He surely couldn't see much in the darkness of the hole, but he must have felt her movement because he let go of her and reached above them to pull the manhole cover shut.

Metal grated against pavement and Levi's body rocked as he muscled the cover back into place above their heads.

Orange fire flashed above them and Isabelle felt its heat penetrate their hiding place.

Levi immediately let go of the manhole cover to shield her. As the simmering air stilled, he slid the manhole cover the last couple of inches closed, leaving them in total darkness. "Are you okay?"

Isabelle could feel herself trembling, but she forced her voice to speak. "Fine. You?"

"Fine," he echoed.

"You didn't scorch your hands, did you?"

"Not too bad."

Isabelle was aware that he hadn't denied being injured, but because he didn't complain, she didn't press the question. It wasn't as though she could do anything for him at the moment.

With the manhole cover blocking out all light, the darkness was damp and absolute, and Isabelle felt a wave of terror wash over her. Who was this man, and what were his intentions? What did the explosions above mean? And where were they? Her nose told her it wasn't the sewer.

"Can you climb down, Princess?" Levi's voice surprised her with its closeness.

Suddenly mindful of her position wrapped in the arms of a man she didn't trust, Isabelle resisted going any farther. Gripping the metal bar a little tighter, she ignored his prompt. "What was that?"

"Ambush." He stated flatly. "Let's get moving."

Isabelle reached upward for the next higher rung. "My family is up there. My brother's car—"

"You're *not* going back up." Levi tugged her back down, closer against him.

The grip of his arms in the darkness brought more horrible memories rushing back. She fought him instinctively. "No! I don't know who you are or what you're doing—"

"Your father hired me to protect you." Levi's arms were too strong for her, and her position on the slippery metal rungs was a precarious one.

She tried to fight back. "The royal motorcade was ambushed and now you're trying to kidnap me. I demand to know why!"

Instead of responding, Levi wrenched her free of the rungs and climbed downward with her more or less slung across his shoulders. "We need to get moving. If the lid on this hole sustains a direct hit, you could be killed standing where you are."

"Where am I?" A shudder of fear chased through her, but Isabelle stopped fighting and relented to being carried down the dark hole. She felt the vibrations as another explosion rocked the earth in spite of the thick stone that surrounded them, so she didn't doubt Levi's warning was sincere.

"The Catacombs of Charlemagne."

Isabelle startled and nearly fell out of Levi's arms. He obviously hadn't expected her to jolt at his words.

"We're in the Catacombs of Charlemagne?"

"Yes."

"But they were filled in more than a thousand years ago." Her words, spoken in an awed whisper, echoed through the empty chamber.

"Your father had them excavated." Levi climbed downward, his movements slow and deliberate in the darkness.

"How do *you* know that, and *I* don't?" Isabelle couldn't fathom why her father hadn't told her. And how had Levi learned of them?

"I was just wondering the same thing." Levi's voice echoed louder, and Isabelle realized the chamber had widened with their descent. He continued. "Actually, your great-grandfather King Alexander III began the excavation during the first World War, thinking the royal family might need the catacombs to escape if they were ever threatened on their own soil." His posture changed as he let go of the ladder, and Isabelle heard the scraping sound of his shoes against the floor of the tunnel. "Little did your great-grandfather know, he was right—just a century off."

Isabelle wished she could see his face, but the utter darkness hid everything. So much had happened so quickly, she wasn't sure she entirely understood what Levi was talking about. "The catacombs run beneath the city of Sardis." She recalled from history lessons. "Charlemagne built them in the ninth century when he used Lydia as an outpost in his attempt to further his kingdom and the spread of Christianity toward the east."

In a patient-sounding voice, Levi continued the story. "Lydia has always been a Christian nation, so they supported Charlemagne's efforts."

"Even though he was eventually thwarted." Isabelle wasn't sure how large a space they occupied, but from the way their voices carried, she judged it to be at least a few meters wide, with a ceiling well above their heads. Tentatively she stepped away from Levi, half expecting to feel cold stone against her back. She felt nothing. With a shiver, she took a step back toward him, unwilling to lose her only human contact in the vast darkness.

"Stay near me." He cautioned her abruptly. "We need to get moving."

Isabelle gulped a breath of the cool underground air. She had to think. Too much about this situation wasn't right, and just because the man knew about the catacombs, that didn't mean she ought to trust him. After all, there was surely little coincidence between the timing of his appointment and the attack on the royal motorcade. For all she knew he was in on the ambush and had brought her into the tunnel to finish her off or hand her over to a political enemy.

But how could she sort out what to do when she couldn't even see?

Levi tugged on her arm.

"Hold on." Isabelle pulled her cell phone from her purse and flicked it open, illuminating the screen, its miniscule light startling in the utter darkness of the tunnel, casting their faces and the rock walls around them in an eerie green-ish glow.

"Thank you. That helps." Levi offered her a slight smile.

To Isabelle, his angled lips looked sinister in the flickering light. "You should take your sunglasses off."

As she watched his face, his jaw tightened under his close-cropped beard. He seemed reluctant to remove the mirrored shades, which, together with the facial hair, hid his face almost completely. At his hesitation, Isabelle realized she'd never seen him without the sunglasses on, not even indoors. For a moment, she wondered why.

Then he slowly peeled back the lenses and she knew the answer.

Not everyone in Lydia had brown eyes, but the majority of the people did. The country was located west of Macedonia, where the heel of the boot of Italy split the Adriatic and Ionian seas. Most native Lydians, like the people of Greece and the rest of the Mediterranean region, had olive complexions, dark hair and dark brown eyes.

As Levi pulled off his sunglasses, she saw that his eyes were blue.

She couldn't suppress her startled gasp. If Levi wasn't Lydian, how had he come to work for the royal bodyguard? The law required every member of the Lydian military to be a citizen—and no one could serve as a royal bodyguard without first serving at least four years in the military. By what deception had Levi tricked her father into hiring him? And what was he planning to do with her?

She realized he still had hold of her arm, and she wished there was some way she could pull away and nonchalantly put some distance between them. But Levi remained close to her in their small circle of light. Fear found its way into her voice. "The royal bodyguard draws its team from the elite of the Lydian military forces. Only citizens of Lydia can join the military."

"I am a citizen of Lydia."

"How is that possible?"

"My mother is Lydian. My father is American."

Isabelle felt her eyes narrow. Was he baiting her? Her father, King Philip of Lydia, had married an American—her mother, Queen Elaine. But it was a rare combination, and she found it doubly suspicious that she and Levi had something so unique in common. "Who do you work for?"

"The Lydian government." Impatience flickered in his blue eyes. "We should get moving."

"I don't trust you."

His expression relaxed slightly. "I sensed that. If you will agree to keep moving, I will explain a bit more of who I am and what I know of this afternoon's attack."

Isabelle's mouth opened slightly as she weighed her answer. Should she move farther into the darkness with this stranger? Every warning bell inside her clamored against it. Yet really, what choice did she have? Surely only danger waited above them. "Where are we going? What about my family? They were up there in the motorcade—"

"We can't do anything to help them now. You have a responsibility as a member of the royal family not to endanger yourself, correct?"

"Yes." Isabelle felt her shoulders droop with resignation. How many times had her parents reminded her of that fact? Every time she left the country—every time she'd ever tried to do anything on her own. Even her humanitarian work overseas was often hampered by her royal obligation to her own safety.

"Then you can't go back up. We can only go forward." He looked down at the dim light from her cell phone. "We should save the battery. Close that—we can walk in darkness."

A protest rose to Isabelle's lips, but she doubted it would do her any good to voice her fears. Levi was right about the light. There was nothing more for it to illumine—just the stone walls of the catacomb, and they could feel their way along those well enough. Surely the light would become more urgently necessary in the future. He was wise to advise her not to waste it.

She snapped the phone shut and the light went out, leaving them in total darkness again. "Explain, then. Who are you? And what just happened up there?"

Levi cupped her elbow with one hand. In the total silence of the tunnel she could hear his other hand skimming along the wall as they moved cautiously down the cobbled floor. The blue-eyed bodyguard began his story.

"My father works for a Christian organization called Sanctuary International. Their primary mission is to help religious refugees find asylum. Thirty-five years ago, when he was working in the Balkan region, he formed close ties with your father. Lydia is one of the few countries in the region where religious freedom is zealously defended, and your father proved to be an invaluable ally.

"During that time, my father and mother met and were married, but they returned to the United States before I was born. I received dual Lydian-U.S. citizenship through my parents, and though I was raised in the United States, I often spent summers visiting my grandparents in Lydia."

Levi paused. "The wall curves away," he murmured, "and I suspect it forks."

Before he finished speaking Isabelle had her phone out, and its tiny light illuminated the two branching tunnels gaping open in endless darkness. The bodyguard glanced between them before nodding. "This way." He didn't hesitate to step forward down the right-hand branch.

"Why this way?"

"After two more turns we will be below the Sardis Cathedral. It should be safe to exit there."

"How do you know the catacombs so well?" Isabelle closed her phone reluctantly, still suspicious of his motives in spite of his story.

"I've been studying them for the past six days."

"Why?"

Levi seemed to struggle with how to answer her. Once again, Isabelle's suspicions were raised. Was he really who he said he was? Did the history he told her really happen, or was he simply making it up to placate her until the rest of his nefarious plans could be accomplished?

His answer seemed to come in a roundabout way. "Our aid workers in the region have formed close ties with many Christians with diverse political ties. Six days ago, an informant delivered a coded message at a Sanctuary outpost on the Albanian border. The next morning his body was found floating in the Mursia River."

Isabelle found that her steps had slowed as she listened closely to Levi's explanation. "What did the coded message say?" She shivered a little as she stepped tentatively through the darkness, uncertain whether she really wanted to know the answer to her question.

Apology and regret filled Levi's voice. "It contained instructions for an attack on the royal family."

"Today's attack?"

"Presumably. It did not give a date or time. That's why I immediately replaced your usual bodyguard."

"I don't understand."

"The message was supposed to be delivered to Alfred, the man who was scheduled to guard you today. He was apparently a member of this insurgent organization. The message contained instructions. As soon as the first explosion detonated, Alfred was supposed to kill you."

TWO

Levi didn't like sharing the details of the planned attack with Isabelle. He didn't want to cause her any more distress than she'd already experienced. But because she didn't trust him, he didn't know how else to impress upon her the gravity of her circumstances. Whether she trusted him or not, he needed her to follow his every instruction. Their lives would depend on it.

Now the princess stumbled and Levi held her arm more firmly to steady her.

"Alfred?" Isabelle repeated, disbelief in her tone. "He's been part of my guard for four years."

"I know, and a member of the royal army for sixteen years before that. We have been unable to determine when he joined the insurgents."

"Where is he now?" Isabelle asked. "I should hope he was arrested and questioned."

"He was floating in the Mursia next to the man who brought us the message."

"Yet the insurgents still went through with the attack? If they knew enough to kill those men, they had to have known the note was intercepted."

Levi could only guess at what their original plans might have been. "Perhaps they thought the longer they waited, the more time we would have to prepare a defense."

"But if my father knew about this, why did my family stay in Lydia? Why didn't we leave the moment the message was intercepted?"

With his head bent a little closer to hers in the darkness, Levi wished he could study the face of the princess entrusted to his care. "Surely you know the answer to that question."

A resigned sigh was Isabelle's only indication of emotion. "My father would never leave the throne. It would signal to the insurgents that he was a coward."

Levi nodded. "They would see it as an open door to walk through and take the country."

"Then why weren't my brother and sister and I at least sent away? Why were we all in the same motorcade?"

"The three of you were originally supposed to be riding in the same car," Levi reminded her. "Your father refused to call off the state dinner for the same reason he would never run away from his throne." Levi had begged the king to send his children away for their own safety, but he understood King Philip's reasons for keeping them there. They had argued about it well into the night. Levi was still exhausted from missing sleep.

Now he answered the princess patiently. "Your father believed that, with the message intercepted, the insurgents would change their plans and call off their attack. He feared that if he tried to send you away, they would see it as a sign of weakness and instead attack with greater force. He thought this would be the best way to keep you safe."

Isabelle trembled. Levi realized that, on top of all that had happened, the damp cold of the catacombs was probably getting to her. With only narrow straps instead of sleeves, her dress surely did little to keep her warm.

As her regal posture sagged under the weight of all she'd absorbed, Levi slid off his tuxedo jacket and nestled it around her shoulders. He, too, feared for her family and what may have happened to them. She had surely guessed their fate, and Levi had no reassurances to give her. There was really very little hope for the Royal House of Lydia.

"We should keep moving," he said softly after her trembling had given way to sniffling. "If we can reach other Sanctuary team members, perhaps they will have good news about your family."

"Maybe I should try calling them."

Levi sucked in a breath.

"Why not?" Isabelle pulled back from him.

"We don't know who would answer your call, and we can't risk the wrong people finding out where you are. For the same reason, I have no intention of using my phone until we reach a safe location. If Alfred was working for the insurgents, anyone could be." He urged her on. "The best thing we can do right now is get you out of here."

The princess took several deep breaths but made no move to head forward.

"You still don't trust me?" he asked.

"I trusted Alfred."

Levi nodded. "Perhaps you are wise not to trust me." Her long hair, which had been piled high in an artful arrangement for the state dinner, had come loose, and a thick strand brushed his hand. "Can you open the light?"

She clicked her phone open, and her wide brown eyes stared fearfully up at him in its thin glow. Gently he pushed the loose hair back from her eyes.

"Your hands were burned," she accused him as his fingers passed through her line of vision.

"I hadn't meant for you to notice," he apologized. "There is nothing we can do for them here."

The princess straightened, as though drawing from a well of courage only a royal could tap. "Then we must get to a first aid kit. Let's hurry."

Levi took her cue and turned them down the next tunnel, which would lead under the centuries-old Cathedral where many Lydian saints were buried. The church had been built upon the rumored burial place of the original Lydia, an early leader in the Christian church whose conversion by the Apostle Paul was detailed in the sixteenth chapter of the Book of Acts in the Bible. The nation of Lydia had been named for her house church, and the royal family, including Isabelle herself, could trace their roots back to Lydia's family.

It was a reminder to Levi of the amazing lineage of the woman who held their only light as they walked through the darkness of the catacombs. Though he had long respected Isabelle from afar as he'd read about her humanitarian efforts as a princess, he was even more impressed with her in person. And she was even more beautiful than the newspaper photos he'd seen.

"Which way?" Isabelle asked when they arrived at the next fork in the tunnel.

It was a good question. Levi had studied hand-drawn maps of the tunnels, which were known only to a select few. Because King Philip had supplied the maps, Levi had assumed the whole royal family would be familiar with the layout of the catacombs. It surprised him that Isabelle was unaware of their very existence. Now he tried to recall the detailed twists and turns of the elaborate underground labyrinth.

The light from Isabelle's phone dimmed. "Do you know which way it is?"

Finally able to picture he map in his head, Levi pulled her a little closer to him as they headed down the left-hand passageway. "This way, but let's leave the light off if we can. We might need it more later."

To his relief, Isabelle didn't argue with him but shuffled along beside him as they made their way down the tunnel in dizzying darkness. He could only hope she would cooperate with him for as long as it might take to get her to safety. Their situation was difficult enough, and Levi desperately needed the mission to be successful.

Not only did he care about his mother's home country and feel allegiance toward the Royal House of Lydia, but he also had a very personal reason why the mission could *not* fail. His father didn't just work for Sanctuary International, he was its president. And he'd be retiring in another year. Everyone expected Nicolas Grenaldo to appoint one of his two sons to be president after him.

And that was just the trouble. Although Levi had spent four years in the Lydian army before going on to law school, he didn't have any battle experience. He'd studied international law, thinking at the time it would give him the best possible background for leading an organization that helped people throughout the world. Too late he'd realized no amount of studying would earn him the respect and admiration of his peers within Sanctuary.

His little brother, Joe, however, had spent six years in the United States Marine Corps, followed by several successful and high-profile operations with Sanctuary. Joe had saved the lives of dozens of missionaries, political figures and refugees over the years.

Levi had saved no one. As the older brother, he should have been the natural choice to follow in his father's footsteps. But as of right now, Joe was everyone's favorite. Joe was a hero. Levi desperately needed this mission to go well if he wanted his father to see him as anything other than a scholar. And for that to happen, he'd have to have Isabelle's cooperation.

The darkness was so complete it made his eyes hurt. Levi had almost begun to wonder if he'd missed the stairs when a gap in the wall left him grasping into the open air.

He stopped.

Isabelle snapped her light on just long enough to display a twisting set of stone stairs that curled upward and out of sight. Then she let the light die again before stepping forward onto the first stair.

"Wait," Levi whispered, tugging her back. "We need to discuss our next step."

As he pulled her back, she brushed near him, and this time, with her standing one step higher on the stone stairs, he felt her lose hair brush past his cheek and smelled her flowery fragrance, so different from the dank catacombs. He swallowed, refusing to allow himself to think about how close she was to him.

Levi had always known Isabelle was a beautiful woman, but he was in her life for a short time only, to fulfill a specific mission. He would behave with absolute decorum. She was, after all, a princess. And he'd been briefed privately by her father about the horrors of her failed engagement. Sympathy and respect stifled his otherwise-strong sense of attraction toward her.

She must have realized how close she'd gotten to him in the darkness because he felt her back away. He doubted she felt anything near the kind of attraction he did, but then, she'd already said she didn't trust him. Perhaps it was best that way.

"What is your plan?" Isabelle asked.

He could feel the warmth of her breath on his cheek and realized she hadn't backed too far away from him after all. Still holding her arm with one hand, he analyzed their options.

"We don't know if the insurgents are aware of the catacombs or of the opening below the cathedral. I would assume not, but—" He hesitated.

"I would assume nothing, under the circumstances."

Levi agreed. "We'll make our way up the stairs in silence.

I've never been through this way so I don't know what we'll find at the end."

"Is it even passable?"

"Yes. Your father wouldn't have allowed it to be marked as an exit if it wasn't passable. But because we don't know if it's a sealed door or if your light will show—"

"I'll keep my light off."

"Good. Given the possibility of danger ahead, we can't risk giving away our presence."

"Extreme caution." Isabelle concurred, and he could feel her head nod in the darkness.

Levi was acutely aware of the slight movement. She'd slowly allowed herself to lean closer to him. Did she realize how close to one another they now stood in the dark chamber? He tried not to think about his proximity to the princess.

The pressing danger provided excellent distraction. "We'll proceed with extreme caution," he echoed. "If at any point we encounter any person or anything that seems out of the ordinary, we'll halt and assess the situation. If danger is apparent, we'll retreat back the way we came."

"And if we cannot retreat into the catacombs?" The princess tipped her head forward as she spoke, and Levi felt the softness of her hair come to rest near his jaw.

Levi didn't feel he ought to push her away, yet the floral perfume she wore teased his nostrils. "Then God help us."

Isabelle pulled back from him.

The cold air of her absence cleared his mind. He realized how his words must have sounded and rushed to explain. "We don't know the size of the forces the insurgents have attacked with. If they take the cathedral and block our passage to the catacombs, then it would mean they've completely overwhelmed your father's government, in which case I don't know how we could possibly get you out of the country alive."

"Out of the country?" Isabelle backed farther away from him this time. "You said my father didn't want me leaving the country, that it would send the wrong message to the insurgents."

"That was before the attack," Levi corrected her. "You can't expect to stay—"

"I will not leave!"

Levi's hand flew out to cover her mouth. "Shh," he hushed her, aware of how loudly her voice had echoed. She squirmed away from him. He hadn't intended to clamp his hand over her royal mouth, but he couldn't risk letting her voice give away their location when they didn't know who might hear.

Cautiously he removed his hand.

Isabelle whispered angrily. "You said my father wished to avoid any sign of weakness—"

"They think you're *dead.*" He tried to reach for her shoulder to pull her back so he could reason with her, but she batted him away. "Princess Isabelle." He spoke her name with caution.

"The Royal House of Lydia is not dead. We live and we reign."

Levi was reminded by the emotion in her words that she'd been raised with a profound sense of duty toward her people, an obligation of leadership that had been deeply ingrained since birth. It wasn't in her to run away when her government was challenged. How could he make her understand that she *had* to do just that?

"Yes." He spoke in the most soothing voice he could muster. "Yes, Lydia is ruled by your family, by the Royal House of Lydia."

"I am *not* dead," she choked.

He realized she was weeping. He didn't blame her one bit. "You're not dead," he repeated, trying to think of what he could possibly say that wouldn't make her more upset. What was there to say? It was likely the rest of her family had been killed. She had surely guessed that much already. As soon as the insurgent forces realized she had escaped, they'd come looking for her. But he couldn't tell her that—not now—so he tried to reassure her as best he could.

"You're not dead, Princess. You're alive, and I will do everything in my power to keep you alive. But right now we don't know what the situation is out there. If the insurgents have taken control of the city—"

"No!" Isabelle moved to push past him again. "No, they *cannot* take the city." She turned as though she was going to stomp right up the stairs and demand to have rule returned to her.

"Isabelle." He pulled her back against him and this time held her tight so she couldn't do anything rash. He pressed his mouth near her ear as he had in the car and spoke calmly but forcefully. "The insurgents want you dead. As long as they think they have already killed you, they won't come looking for you. If they learn you're really alive, they'll hunt you down. Your only hope for survival is to stay out of sight and get out of Lydia as quickly as possible—before they have time to search for your dead body and wonder why they can't find it."

"But the Royal House of Lydia has never given over control of the country. It is my royal duty—"

"It's your duty to stay *alive*." As he held her tightly, he felt some of the fight leave her. "You can't reclaim the throne if you're dead. If you let me get you out of here, we can negotiate your rightful return to the throne."

"How can I run from my people like a coward?"

"Your only other option is to face near-certain death. Who will defend your people then?"

He felt her war with that decision as he held her, his arms

still firmly rooting her in place lest she suddenly take off up the stairs.

Finally she told him in a determined voice, "I still don't trust you."

"It doesn't matter if you trust me. All I ask is that you allow me to protect you."

A huff erupted from her nose, and her chin lifted off from where it had come to rest on his shoulder. "Have I made it that difficult for you?"

"You did seem determined to stay in the car long enough for the insurgents to hit it."

"If you would have told me about the catacombs earlier—"

"I didn't know you didn't know," he defended. He relaxed his hold enough to let her move half an arm's length away but no farther. He still didn't trust her any more than she trusted him. "There may be moments up ahead when I don't have time to explain everything. Whether you trust me or not, you need to follow my lead. If I have to stop and argue with you at every turn, it will give the insurgents an unfair advantage. I fear we must move very quickly."

Her shoulders rose and fell under his hands as she took a deep breath. "Up the stairs in darkness, through the cathedral and then what?"

"The U.S. Embassy is across the street. They should be able to help us get out of the country."

Isabelle was silent. Levi could tell she was weighing her response. Based on the background information he'd been given, he could guess at what might be the cause of her silence.

"I know you don't care for the American ambassador," Levi began.

"Stephanos Valli remains in this country solely to retain the good will of the American government. If it were up to

me, he would never be allowed to set foot in Lydia again."
Her words seethed with barely repressed anger.

"We need the Americans to help us get you out of the
country alive. If Valli was headed to the state dinner, it's
likely he won't be anywhere near the embassy. His staff can
get us out of the country." Levi had never met Stephanos
Valli, but he understood that the American ambassador had
Lydian ancestry and ties to the most powerful people in their
area of the Mediterranean. Valli had negotiated the engagement of the princess to one of those people, a billionaire businessman named Tyrone Spiteri. The engagement had ended
in scandal. Levi had never been told the details, but he understood Isabelle's bitterness toward the ambassador for his
hand in such an embarrassing experience.

And Isabelle obviously wasn't ready to risk an encounter
with Valli, though it had been two years since her engagement to Tyrone Spiteri had ended. "I have many friends who
could possibly help us," she suggested.

"Do you know them better than you knew Alfred?"

She tensed, and Levi could feel her head shaking regretfully in the darkness.

"I suppose," she whispered softly, "we can't trust anyone
because we can't be sure of whose side they're on."

"The Americans should be trustworthy."

"Perhaps." For a moment she sounded overwhelmed, but
she seemed to draw quickly from that royal well of strength.
"Let's get moving then. I still intend to find a first aid kit if
we can."

Levi was impressed with how quickly she made up her
mind and how silently she made her way up the stairs. He
counted seven, eight, nine steps before his head knocked into
something solid.

"Stop," he whispered quietly as a breath while moving to
shield her head.

His burned fingers were momentarily squeezed between her high-piled hair and the obstruction. Tears sprang to his eyes but he stifled an exclamation. Finding her ear beside him, he whispered, "There's an obstruction above us. It may be a trap door. I'm going to try to lift up."

He eased his shoulders up against it, but even when he began to apply greater force, nothing budged.

"Does it have a latch of some sort?" Isabelle whispered back. He could feel her hands skirt past him in the darkness, and a moment later he heard a soft click. "Try it now," she whispered.

This time when Levi applied pressure upward, the ceiling moved silently, though the space above seemed to be just as dark as the tunnel they'd come from. With only a slight rustle from her evening gown, Isabelle slid through the opening, and Levi followed after her, closing the door softly after they were both out.

Isabelle's hand traveled up his arm, and he felt her fingers tug on his earlobe. At her prompt he leaned down and she whispered silently into his ear. "Should I try my light?"

Feeling for her hands, he covered the light, then nodded. "Go ahead."

The light came on and slowly he allowed more of its miniscule glow to shine. The two of them looked around at the statues and marble plaques, their blank-eyed stone faces deeply shadowed.

Isabelle shivered at the sight of the stone faces, whose forms hid the ancient bones of her ancestors. "The mausoleum," she whispered. They'd toured it once when she was very young, but no one had been buried under the cathedral in several generations, so she'd had no cause to visit it again. Her sole impression was that it was a frightening place cluttered with dead upon dead, which seemed to go on forever.

But then, she'd been only about eight years old when she'd made that tour. Surely it wouldn't be so frightening now that she was twenty-four.

Her light dimmed, and she snapped the phone shut again. Although complete darkness shrouded everything from her sight, she was acutely aware of the looming stone figures and tried not to imagine their blank eyes staring back at her through the darkness. She had to remember that the insurgent threat against her was far more real than her fears of the dark and the dead.

"Do you know your way around in here?" Levi asked in a hushed whisper.

"No. Do you?"

"I've never been down here before."

"I visited once, but it was a long time ago. All I really remember is…" The memories stumbled through her mind, tripping over themselves like the patent-leather shoes she and her sister had worn as they traveled hand-in-hand through the tour, nearly running in the end, chased by fear, wanting only to find the sunlight. She stepped instinctively closer to Levi, the only human figure in the room who lived and breathed. "I didn't like it."

"Do you know which way we should go?"

Isabelle searched the long-buried memory, sorting through the fright to find some tidbit that could help them. "We came in through the back of the church and came out at the front. The mausoleum runs the length of the cathedral, with family crypts branching off on either side." She pulled his tuxedo jacket more tightly around her. "Most of these bones are more than a thousand years old. No was has been buried here in generations."

"So we should try to find the central hallway?"

"That much shouldn't be difficult. Then we go one way or the other. The trick will be not to get sidetracked, or we could end up wandering around here—" Her voice broke off as she heard a distant boom, the first sound to penetrate the deathly stillness.

"The trick will be to avoid detection." Levi's words were spoken in a near-silent breath by her ear.

Isabelle also tensed, listening to the sound Levi had obviously heard. Distantly, echoes reverberated through the still air. Footsteps? And muffled voices.

"Search every corner." The command rose above the sound of footsteps—many sets of footsteps. Someone was in the mausoleum looking for them!

Isabelle grabbed Levi's arm and whispered, "What are we going to do now?"

"The footsteps are all coming from the same direction. We need to run the other way."

Isabelle raised her hand to open her phone again and light their way, but Levi's fingers quickly closed over hers.

"No. No light."

"I can't see where I'm going." Isabelle protested in near-silence as Levi tugged her along beside him.

"No light," Levi repeated. "It will lead them straight to us."

They shuffled forward, and Isabelle couldn't help but wonder if they weren't leaving a trail of footprints for their pursuers to follow. But tourist groups went through the mausoleum several times a week, if not several times a day. Hopefully their footprints would blend in.

For a few moments they bumped along in darkness, here and again meeting the rounded sides of cold stone statues or the walls themselves. Then Isabelle's peering eyes were shocked as the bulbs that ran along the central hallway illuminated.

"They've turned the lights on," she whispered softly, her

words nearly drowned by the echoes of boots on stone floor and the muffled shouts of the approaching men.

Because the branching crypts weren't lighted, she turned toward the light of the central hallway.

Levi pulled back on her arm. "They'll see you."

"But we're sitting ducks in here. There's no way out of this chamber unless we get to the main hallway."

Already the boom of footsteps pounded closer. She didn't know how thoroughly the men were searching the sprawling chambers, but they were closing in on them.

"We'll have to hide."

Isabelle looked around. The life-size statues were almost big enough to hide behind.

Almost.

"Where?"

Levi's fingers grasped the edge of one of the many marble slabs that rested on the raised ledges of the burial chambers. Isabelle watched as he slid back the solid stone slab.

"In here."

The boom of footsteps echoed nearer.

"No." Isabelle shook her head. "Not with the bones."

Levi pulled an object from the vault. "They're not bones." He held out an ancient piece of wood for her to see.

"It's a shuttle," Isabelle realized. She recalled from her long-ago tour that the burial chambers were interspersed with vaults containing items important to the deceased. Since weaving and textile work had long been the basis for the Lydian economy, many weavers treasured their looms and shuttles—even to the point of being buried with the objects that had been an integral part of their livelihood.

Realizing the chamber Levi had opened didn't hold any bones, she relented to hiding inside. Levi guided her feet-first through the opening.

"Hurry!" he encouraged her as the echoing footfalls drew closer.

"Did you hear that?" A deep voice echoed down the corridor.

"This way!"

The boom of boots on stone grew louder and faster as the men hurried toward them.

With a repentant gulp, Isabelle ducked into the hole, regretting that her hesitation had wasted precious seconds.

"Up ahead!" the men's voices called, nearer this time. Almost upon them.

Isabelle shuffled her head around so she could look out of the opening. Levi's face flashed across her line of vision. "Are you coming in?" she whispered.

"No time," he mouthed, shoving the stone slab nearly shut, leaving her with just a slice of light before he spun around.

THREE

Levi ducked instinctively as the bullet ricocheted through the stone chamber. He gripped the shuttle he'd pulled from the chamber, its ancient wood petrified with age. It wasn't much of a weapon, but it in the enclosed space it would be far more useful to him than the gun in his holster.

"Don't discharge your weapons inside the mausoleum!" The commanding voice Levi had heard earlier now sounded like it was just around the next corner. "The bullets could bounce back and hit one of us."

The sound of footsteps drew nearer and flashlight beams danced through the relative darkness of the side chamber. Levi leapt back, hiding in the shadow of a large statue nearest the opening of the chamber on the side from which the voices approached.

He gripped the shuttle as the footsteps boomed nearer.

The instant a shadow fell across the opening Levi leapt forward and struck with the petrified rod. The man crumpled to the floor with a hollow groan.

"What—" The next soldier stepped forward, and Levi hit him, a glancing blow across the back of the head, which appeared to stun him only slightly. He grimaced and gathered himself, but Levi caught him under the jaw with his other fist. He slumped over his fallen comrade.

Two down. How many more to go?

With a shout, another solider leapt over the two unconscious figures. Levi swung with the shuttle, but the man's hand clamped his wrist. A high round kick cleared the two motionless men below them. He caught his attacker under the ribs.

He heard the air rush from the man's lungs as the soldier leaned forward, his grip easing on Levi's wrist.

Jerking his arm free, Levi caught the man in the back of his head before he straightened.

Just in time.

The soldier went down as another leaped forward. At the rate he was going, Levi would soon have the entrance to the side chamber blocked by the unconscious bodies of his attackers. This soldier's feet hadn't yet hit the floor when Levi caught him under the chin with a grunt, with the same motion heaving his body onto the growing pile.

He panted, trying to catch his breath. His singed hands stung. How many more soldiers were there? How many more could he hold off?

The crackle of a radio told him someone was about to give away his position.

Vaulting the heap of men, Levi knocked the radio from the man's hand before the soldier could call in reinforcements. Grabbing his head by the helmet, Levi rammed the man face-first into his knee.

Three soldiers were still standing.

The nearest one spun sideways, clipping Levi in a blow to the chest.

Levi grasped the shuttle with both hands and brought it down on the man's head.

The soldier shuddered and went down.

"Alec?" The next guy looked at him in confusion.

Levi didn't recognize the young man. "Sorry," Levi apologized as he slugged the soldier across the jaw.

Before he had time to pull his arm back, the next man was on top of him, knocking him flat. Levi just managed to catch himself enough to avoid hitting his head too hard against the stone floor, but he wasn't quick enough to avoid the blow aimed at the side of his head.

Stars flashed across his field of vision, obliterating all else. Levi shoved back, trying to push the man off of him, to roll sideways, anything. But he was exhausted from what had already been a long fight against overwhelming odds, and this attacker was enormous.

The man on top of him had every advantage.

Levi braced himself and prayed.

Suddenly the man shuddered, falling on top of him.

With a whoosh, the weight of the oversize soldier knocked what remained of Levi's breath from his lungs.

He groaned as he attempted to heave the deadweight figure off of him.

A small, neatly manicured hand appeared, hefting the man by the shoulder, adding just enough lift to allow Levi to push the man off to the side. As his vision cleared, Levi looked up to find Princess Isabelle smiling down at him.

"How did you—?" he started to ask.

She held up another shuttle like a royal scepter. "There were two of these."

Levi moaned and sat up. "But how did you get the stone rolled back from the inside?"

Motioning with the shuttle, Isabelle imitated how she'd levered the shuttle through the opening to move back the stone. "Simple tools," she said, glancing back at the heap of men behind her as a groan rumbled from the bottom of the pile. "We should get out of here."

"Sure." Levi leapt up and, with a quick kick in the direction from which the groan had come, muttered, "That should keep him quiet." He plucked up the radio that had flown free when he'd knocked out the man who was trying to use it. "Let's go before anyone else realizes what just happened."

Isabelle hesitated. "Do we want to take their guns? We don't want these guys to be armed when they wake up—especially if it takes us a while to get out of here."

Although he didn't want to waste the time it would take to do so, Levi had to admit Isabelle's idea was a good one. The men could very well awaken before he got the princess through the cathedral and safely across the street to the American Embassy. "Okay, but let's be quick about it."

Levi grabbed the guns, stuffing several of them into the vault where Isabelle had hidden, before closing the stone seal. He then hurried to empty the soldiers' pockets of anything that might be useful before slinging an assault rifle over his shoulder.

Isabelle grabbed a flashlight from one of the prone figures. "These men are Lydian soldiers. I might have thought they were after me to protect me if they hadn't fired a shot at us." Her features clouded. The soldiers had betrayed their vow to protect the royal family.

But why?

Much as he didn't want to think about it, he knew the question needed to be voiced. "Whose orders were they following?"

Concern filled Isabelle's face. "As king, my father is the head of the Lydian military, but if any of the commanders had turned—" Her words broke off, the situation clearly catching up to her.

"Someone issued a command for these soldiers to come down here looking for us."

"Do you think they knew who they were looking for? Every soldier takes a vow upon enlistment to serve and protect the royal family. They must not have known they'd been sent after me."

Levi sensed her struggle as she considered what the presence of the soldiers meant. Did the soldiers know who they'd been sent after? He didn't have time to sort it out.

"We need to get moving. These men could wake up any moment."

With the bright lights shining down from the hallway ceiling above them, they ran the length of the hall, finding the door to the stairs still open where the soldiers had entered.

"Do you think it's safe?" Isabelle asked in a breathless voice.

Levi listened carefully but heard no sound above them. "I imagine the men were dispersed in teams to search the area surrounding the ambush. The cathedral is only about three blocks from where the motorcade stopped. It will take them a while to canvass the area. I doubt anyone will come back to this building until they realize our men downstairs haven't checked in."

"I hate to think they'd be organized enough to make that realization very quickly." Isabelle's intelligent eyes looked up at him intently, her loose lock of hair tumbling down and brushing his hand again. He doubted she was even aware of it, yet it did terrible things to his focus.

Her determined expression took his breath away. He knew she was shaken by all that had happened—she'd wept not very long ago—but here she was, already dealing capably with the situation. And she'd saved his life with that shuttle.

He swallowed, struggling to think what to say next. What had they been talking about? The woman was far too beautiful. As soon as he got her to safety he'd hand her off to someone else. She was difficult to work with—for all the wrong reasons.

Before he could gather his scattered thoughts, Isabelle

surprised him by scooping up one of his singed hands into her much smaller fingers.

"Before we go any farther, we should pray," she said softly, pinching her eyes shut and bowing her head without waiting for a response from him.

"Lord God, Protector of Lydia, Sovereign of our Nation and Lord of the Universe." In her royal way, she began with God's majestic titles before pleading for protection—not just for them, but for the rest of her family. "Wherever my parents and siblings are, I know that You are with them. In Your infinite mercy, watch over them. Keep us all safe until You bring us together once again. Amen."

Levi also offered an amen and half expected Isabelle to linger after her prayer, but she didn't even look at him before she headed through the doorway. It took Levi another second before he realized he would have to hurry to keep up with the woman he'd been hired to protect.

Isabelle proceeded as quickly as she dared up the stone steps to the main back hall of the cathedral. She knew the way to the front entrance, having worshipped regularly at the ancient church since she was an infant. Not only did she want to make up for the time they'd lost already, but she felt the need to stay ahead of Levi. He'd begun to make her feel uncomfortable.

She was used to having bodyguards. They'd gone everywhere with her all her life. They were a part of her life.

But she'd never prayed with one before, never clung to one like she'd held on tight to Levi as she'd fought him, cowered in fear with him and wept with him.

Sure, she was plenty used to bodyguards. But she wasn't remotely used to getting that close to a man—any man. The very thought made her recall the final terrified minutes of her failed engagement. Tyrone's face popped into her mind—the face of the man she'd wanted so much to love, the man who had only wanted to take advantage of her.

The hard-learned lesson dug itself a little deeper into her heart. She hadn't even suspected Tyrone's true motives until it had almost been too late. Tyrone had been in love with royal power. He'd wanted to marry her for the prestige it would give him.

Her desire to be loved had blinded her so much that she'd almost let him get away with his evil plans. Almost. She would never allow herself to make the same mistake again. She was a princess. Any man who pretended to love her was likely only in love with her royal title. Tyrone hadn't even taken the time to get to know her.

And she'd learned better than to waste her time chasing after love. She shrugged off the unfamiliar feeling of closeness that praying with Levi had caused her to feel. It meant nothing. As soon as she got away from the insurgent threat, she'd figure out how to get away from Levi, too.

They made their way quickly down the ancient stone hallway, which was slightly more worn than the floor of the chambers below but otherwise remarkably similar. Light from the setting sun streamed in through the beveled panes of the antique windows, prisms of vibrant colors splashing them as they ran past.

They reached the front doors, and both of them crouched back against the solid wood, peeking through the clear panes to the scene outside.

The cobbled street and limestone walls looked innocent, as though nothing out of the ordinary had happened in Sardis that day.

Isabelle watched as Levi's hand settled over the door latch.

"Do you think it's safe?" she asked, watching his bearded face carefully.

He pulled his sunglasses from the inside pocket of his

tuxedo jacket as she handed the garment back to him. It would be warm outside. "Safer than in here. The front door of the embassy is less than one hundred meters from where we stand. We'll have to get down the cathedral stairs and up the steps of the Embassy, but we should be able to do it in well under a minute, maybe even thirty seconds if we hurry. That's not long for us to be out in the open."

Isabelle swallowed. "Front door to front door then?"

"That seems like the most expedient route." The mirrored lenses of his sunglasses stayed trained on her face as he slipped on his jacket. "You don't like the plan?"

He could read her that easily? "I don't like the idea of entering Stephanos Valli's turf, even if he's not there." Although three years had passed since Valli had engineered her engagement to Tyrone Spiteri, and two years had gone by since the horrid ending of that engagement, the mere thought of seeing the two-faced ambassador brought her fears and anger back to the surface.

Levi extended one singed hand toward her arm. "I won't let Valli get near you," he promised.

Could it possibly be that simple? Isabelle looked down at the hand whose mere contact with her arm imparted a surprising level of comfort. "We never found any burn ointment for your hands," she realized with regret.

"It's okay. I've made it this far." His hand stayed still on her arm, and Isabelle wished she could see his eyes behind his sunglasses or his face behind the dark outline of his beard. He leaned a little closer. "We should get going. Are you ready?"

Isabelle nodded, clinging to Levi's promise not to let Valli near her. As long as she knew she wouldn't have to face that awful man, they could get to the Embassy and be safe. Finally.

Maybe then she could learn what had become of her parents and siblings. At least she wouldn't have to fear for her life anymore. And she could get away from Levi, whose presence had started making her uncomfortable for all sorts of new reasons, mostly because he'd gotten so close to her.

She straightened and mentally prepared herself for the dash across the street. "Let's go."

"On three," Levi announced, his grip tightening on the door latch. "One, two—" The door swung wide and the two of them burst out, darting in a dead sprint down the steps.

Levi kept one hand on her arm and one hand on the assault rifle he'd lifted from the soldiers. Her heeled pumps offered little in the way of traction, so Isabelle felt grateful to know Levi was ready to catch her if she slipped.

They crossed the street in six strides and Isabelle hoisted the floor-length skirt of her gown as they vaulted the Embassy stairs by twos and threes. Levi swung open the front door and they stepped inside onto the glossy marble floor.

Isabelle looked up, expecting to see the usual uniformed guards that protected the embassy. Instead, Lydian soldiers guarded the entrance. The one nearest her smiled broadly.

"Princess Isabelle, what a pleasant surprise." He and the soldier next to him stepped forward, reaching for their guns. "If you'll hand us your weapons, we'll personally escort you in."

"We'll keep them," Levi said, his presence close behind her reassuring.

Something was wrong. She could feel it. There shouldn't have been Lydian soldiers guarding the door. There shouldn't have been Lydian soldiers in the building at all. Everything felt wrong. Scurrying soldiers stopped as they passed in the hall. What were Lydian soldiers doing in the American Embassy?

Another man in uniform approached them. "You've captured the princess?" he called to his comrades. "Valli will be delighted."

No! Terror squeezed Isabelle's heart as the two guards lunged toward them, their hands stretched out to take their guns.

Levi spun around her, stiff-arming the men in the face with the butt of his rifle before sweeping his other arm around her waist and scooping her up as he shoved his way back through the door. Out of the corner of her eye, Isabelle saw the other officers rushing toward them, pulling out their guns. The heavy doors slammed shut behind them.

Instead of heading back down the stairs and across the open street, Levi surprised her by scooting to the side of the marble landing and leaping over the balustrade into the bushes, taking her with him.

Prickly branches grabbed at her dress as she fell, but the moment her feet hit the firm earth, the branches settled above their heads. Levi shuffled sideways under the cover of the lush Mediterranean foliage.

Above them on the landing she could hear the doors bang open and soldiers shouting, wondering aloud where they'd gone. "Down!" Levi whispered, ushering her toward a window well deep behind the shadows of the landscaping.

Isabelle gulped a breath and jumped. Levi landed silently beside her and immediately grabbed the window by its frame.

"What are you doing?" she whispered, more than aware that the Embassy building was crawling with Lydian soldiers, who were apparently reporting to Valli. "We're breaking back *in?*"

"Shh." Levi pulled the aging window frame from the time-warped wood. "You said you'd trust me."

A blur of responses passed through her mind, most of them involving their near capture moments before, but she bit her tongue and ducked, mindful of the darkness and the cobwebs. The stone room was similar to those in the basement of the cathedral, but instead of bones, it housed cluttered piles of old furniture, discarded desks and slumping stacks of boxes. Levi slid through the window and landed beside her, reaching back up and pulling the wood-framed glass into place behind them.

"Where are we?" She pulled his ear as close to her lips as she could so she wouldn't have to speak above the sound of a breath.

"The basement of the Embassy."

"You brought me straight into the hornets' nest?"

"I'm keeping you alive." He raised the assault rifle in front of his face, covering them as he moved toward the door. "Everyone is outside looking for us."

"So where are we going?"

"The last place they're going to look."

His words were ominous, and Isabelle swallowed, following him down the dark hallway. Unlike the underground mausoleum below the cathedral, the Embassy basement sat at garden level, and the dying sunlight filtered through windows, giving them just enough illumination to find their way through the cluttered space.

They reached a staircase that bent even farther downward, another level below the earth. Isabelle swallowed, her heart thudding in fear. "Do you seriously know where you're going?"

"Of course I do."

"Where?"

"The dungeon." He pulled her close beside him as he took the first step downward.

Isabelle followed, not so much because she trusted him but because she knew for certain, thanks to the comment of the soldier above them, that Valli wanted her captured. If

Levi could prevent that from happening, she'd follow him anywhere, even into a dungeon.

"I just want you to know," she whispered, pulling instinctively closer to him as the filtered light faded to utter darkness, "that I have no intention of hiding in another crypt. That was the most terrifying thing that's happened to me since—" She broke off, thinking.

"Since the soldiers tried to take you to Valli?"

"That was afterward."

"You've had quite a day." He pulled out the small flashlight he'd taken from the soldiers. Its beam cut through the darkness, landing on ancient chains that dripped from the walls. Isabelle tried not to think about the prisoners who'd been shackled inside the dungeon over the years.

"So where are we going?" She couldn't hear any soldiers following them and so assumed it was okay to speak in a normal whisper. It made the darkness feel slightly less oppressive that way.

"Back into the catacombs. From there we can get just about anywhere."

"There's an entrance to the catacombs under the Embassy? Why didn't we come up this way earlier?"

Levi cleared his throat.

Was he buying time before answering? Isabelle wasn't sure, but she didn't like it. Why had he risked their flight across the street if they could have come up through the Embassy?

When Levi finally spoke, his words were less than encouraging. "There's not really an entrance to the catacombs under the Embassy. According to the hand-drawn maps I studied, there used to be one, but it was walled over to prevent the catacombs from being accidentally discovered by the Americans." He reached the back corner of the dungeon and stopped, his light shining against the formidable bricks of the cold stone wall.

Isabelle shuddered, acutely aware of the fix they'd gotten themselves into. The lines of mortar that ran between the stones were dark gray throughout most of the subterranean room, but in the space where Levi shined his light, the mortar looked paler. Fresher. "So what are we supposed to do? Dig our way out?"

"Hold this." Levi handed her the flashlight. "Stand back."

Isabelle obeyed, hoping that whatever Levi was going to do wouldn't take long. What if the soldiers looked behind the bushes and realized they'd come back in through the window? They'd catch up to them quickly if that was the case.

Levi ran his hands along the seams between the large stone bricks. A few grains of mortar crumbled out from between the seams, and he pulled a tool from his pocket, chiseling away at a seam between the stones. Mortar fell like dust. Several hacking motions later, Levi stood back, a satisfied look on his face.

"I need something big and heavy," he murmured, looking around.

"What for?"

"To use as a battering ram."

"You can't possibly expect to force your way through a stone wall."

"It's a false wall," Levi corrected her. "I could probably kick it in, but I don't want to risk an injury."

While he spoke, Isabelle looked around them at the deep underground prison. Like many of the buildings in the millennia-old city, the Embassy had been rebuilt and refurbished many times over the centuries, and discarded building materials cluttered the room. "Here's a beam," she offered, pointing with the flashlight Levi had handed her.

"Good work." Levi snatched it up, hefted the weight of it in his hands and balanced it on his shoulder. "Stand back."

Isabelle did so. She wasn't nearly as sure of Levi's plan as he seemed to be, and she feared that his efforts might bring the ceiling crumbling down on top of them or, at the very least, alert the soldiers to their presence.

The thick end of the old wood thudded against the stones as Levi pummeled it a few times. Then he appeared to brace himself, took several steps back and came at the wall at a run.

"Augh!" Levi exclaimed as the beam buried itself deep in the stones and he stumbled from the impact.

"Shh!" Isabelle hurried to his side. "Are you all right?"

The bodyguard looked stunned as he eased himself to his feet. "I'm fine," he said, though he didn't sound fine. He tugged at the beam and the stones shifted, crumbling away to reveal a round hole half a meter in diameter. The dust settled, exposing utter blackness beyond.

Isabelle shuddered. "Do you think the soldiers won't notice the hole and guess where we've gone?"

Levi pulled off his sunglasses as he turned to face her. His blue eyes were piercing in the silvery beam from the flashlight. "Your father's generals know about the catacombs," he stated bluntly. "They were there when your father shared the maps with me. If Lydian soldiers are answering to Valli, he must have at least one general under his thumb somehow. This tells him nothing he doesn't already know." He reached for her hand. "Would you like to go first?"

Although the hole hardly seemed large enough to squeeze through, Isabelle realized they didn't have time to enlarge it. And the fact that Valli likely knew about the catacombs made their flight that much more urgent.

Reluctantly, Isabelle placed her hand in Levi's and climbed over the pile of rubble to peer into the darkness of the hole.

"You do recall that we left several soldiers in the mausoleum, don't you?"

"I'm sure they've left by now." Levi shined his flashlight into the darkness beyond. "It's less than a meter to the floor. We should hurry."

Realizing he was right, Isabelle hoisted the skirt of her evening gown just high enough to permit her to step through the hole. Her feet found the floor beyond and she secured decent footing among the jumbled stones. As soon as Levi was through she reached for the jacket he wore.

"I'm cold." Even her voice shivered.

Levi pulled off the tuxedo jacket and placed it around her shoulders. "I should have given it to you sooner. I don't need it." His white cotton shirt rose and fell against his muscular chest as he sucked in deep breaths, obviously still winded from the exertion of breaking through the wall.

Slipping her arms through the sleeves, Isabelle turned away from Levi and tried not to think about how indebted she was to the handsome bodyguard for all he'd done on her behalf that evening. Instead she focused on the path ahead.

Isabelle knew they didn't have much ground to cover because the Embassy was so close to the cathedral. They rounded a corner and found themselves back at the staircase that led up to the mausoleum. The climb that had been so frightening the first time now felt familiar, although Isabelle knew they had just as much to fear—possibly more so now that the soldiers knew she was alive. When they lifted the opening above, artificial light continued to shine down brightly from the central hall.

Levi paused. "Do you hear anything?" he asked after some silence.

"Nothing."

"Then let's go."

They clambered through the hole and darted down the

hall. Isabelle saw no sign of the soldiers they'd left behind less than an hour before. Relieved that the men weren't still there, Isabelle nonetheless wondered where they might have gone. Her fingers tightened around Levi's arm, and her steps slowed.

"We need to hurry," he reminded her.

She shook her head. "Hurry where? You said yourself this is the last place they'd likely look for us. If we go running upstairs we could be captured."

The dark line of Levi's beard flexed as he clenched his jaw. He seemed to weigh her words carefully before he spoke. "The soldiers have already checked the cathedral—I have no doubt about that. They'll most likely assume we've fled the area. They'll widen the perimeter of their search area before they recheck where they've already been."

"Do you think so?"

His blue eyes hardened. "Whoever's behind this insurgent uprising, they seem to have gained control of the Lydian military. That means Lydian commanders following Lydian protocol."

Isabelle recalled his earlier insinuation that he'd served in the Lydian military. Although she wanted to question him about it, there simply wasn't time. She followed him down the hallway toward the steps that led up to the cathedral. "How long do you think we'll have before they circle back and check the cathedral again?"

"It depends on how organized they are. They've just pulled off a major ambush so I'd like to believe they won't be too methodical about their search just yet. We might have an hour, maybe several hours. We still need to move quickly."

"And where are we moving to? Do you still think you can get me out of the country?"

A smile twitched in the corner of Levi's eyes. "Now you want out of the country?"

He looked far too pleased with her change of priorities, but Isabelle refused to be distracted from her goal of reaching safety. "If Stephanos Valli is working with the insurgent forces, then yes, I want to get as far from here as I possibly can."

"Then we'll need help." Levi led her up the stairs to the back hallway of the cathedral, where the stone floors gave way to Persian rugs, softening their footfalls. "One of the deacons at the Cathedral is a former Sanctuary International agent. If he's here—if we can find him before anyone else recognizes you—perhaps he can help us get to out of the country. The Sanctuary International headquarters are in New York City. We'll be safest there."

Isabelle nodded. "What does this former agent look like?"

"I don't know," Levi admitted. "We've never met, but your father mentioned his name in passing—"

"What's his name, then?"

"Dan? Don? Dom?"

"Dom Procopio?"

"Yes." Levi snapped his fingers. "I think that's it."

"Dom Procopio is a deacon and a friend of my father," Isabelle offered cautiously. They'd made their way down the richly inlaid hall, and now the doors to the deacons' offices appeared in front of Isabelle as she turned the corner. The name *Dom Procopio* was etched into the placard on the third door, and Isabelle grasped the doorknob with her right hand.

Levi's calloused fingers covered hers. "Careful," he cautioned her, suddenly so close that she could feel his warmth still the goose bumps on her arm. "We don't know what we'll find on the other side of that door."

Isabelle swallowed but didn't dare turn around to meet his eyes. She'd spent too much time getting close to Levi already. Needing to put some space between them, she cautiously cracked the door open just far enough to allow her to see inside the room.

Dom Procopio sat bound to his desk chair, a thick gag stuffed into his mouth.

Isabelle wondered if he was even still alive.

FOUR

Levi hurried to Dom Procopio's side and pulled the gag from the former-agent's mouth. Relief filled him as the older man gasped for breath. The deacon's bulbous eyes rolled as he searched the room and widened when he spotted the princess.

"Your Majesty!" Dom looked as though he would have bowed if he hadn't been tied to the chair. "They said you were dead."

"Not as long as I have any say in the matter." Levi rushed to untie the stubborn knots that bound the man's hands behind his back.

"And who are you?"

When Levi introduced himself and explained that he was an agent with Sanctuary International, the deacon's face brightened immediately.

Isabelle joined Levi at Dom's side, her nimble fingers making quick work of the bindings at his ankles. "Who told you I was dead?"

"It was on the news," Dom gestured with his newly freed hand toward a small television set in the corner of the office. "I heard the explosions outside and tuned in to find out what was happening." He leapt up as soon as Isabelle had freed his feet and switched on the television. Images of smoking vehicles filled the screen. "See for yourself."

Though Levi didn't want Isabelle to have to relive the attack via the breaking news report, at the same time they both needed to know what was going on. He said a silent prayer that nothing on the screen would be too painful for her to see.

But the chaos surrounding the news broadcast provided little in the way of answers.

"All members of the royal family are at this time presumed dead," a solemn-faced reporter announced. Levi recognized the silver-haired man from the local Lydian television station. "Although no bodies have yet been identified, the royal motorcade was destroyed in the ambush, and there is no sign of any surviving member of the royal family."

Levi turned and looked at Isabelle, whose eyes were riveted to the screen. Her lower lip trembled slightly and she pulled his tuxedo jacket tighter around her shoulders.

"I'm sorry," he said, torn between pulling her into an embrace and maintaining an appropriate distance.

The scene on the television split, and half the screen showed an anchor in a newsroom. "Paul," she addressed the on-the-scene reporter, "we've heard rumors of possible sightings of members of the royal family since the blast. There was even a report that Princess Anastasia and a member of the Royal Guard were attacked at the marina. What do you make of these claims?"

"It's difficult to say at this time." Paul's solemn expression became more intent. "The attacks came out of the blue. The scene here on the street is one of disbelief and chaos. All we can say for certain is that none of the bodies have been identified as any member of the royal family."

"No bodies have yet been identified," Isabelle repeated, meeting his eyes. "But they're still assuming I'm dead. Maybe I'm not the only one who escaped." Hope glimmered behind her unshed tears.

Levi realized that Isabelle needed to remain optimistic that her family members might have survived. If she believed them to be dead, she might be immobilized by grief. "Maybe," he concurred. He wished the reporter could tell them who was behind the attacks, but as the footage looped back to the scenes they'd already witnessed, Levi realized it was likely that no one knew any more about what had happened.

He turned his attention back to Dom. "Who tied you up? Soldiers?"

The man's eyes bugged wide. "Lydian soldiers. They asked if I'd seen any members of the royal family. I was shocked because the television said they were all dead."

Isabelle's chin lifted defiantly. "At least one of them escaped."

A warm smile lit Dom Procopio's face. "At least one," he agreed. "And the soldiers didn't specify who they were looking for. Perhaps all of your family is at large."

Levi was grateful to the man for his encouraging words and for the insight he provided. His mind lit upon a detail he'd almost overlooked. "The soldiers we fought earlier in the mausoleum—one of them looked at me and said, 'Alec?'"

He met Isabelle's eyes and she regarded him solemnly for a moment. "Your blue eyes—my brother Alexander has blue eyes. And with your beard covering so much of your face, if the soldiers were looking for my brother, they might have thought you were Alec. He's served many years in the Lydian army. Most of the soldiers know him."

"So your brother may be unaccounted for," Levi concluded.

But Isabelle was clearly thinking about something else. "The soldier in the Embassy, the one who said Valli would be pleased that they'd captured me—he's a friend of my brother. Sergio Cana."

"Do you think Sergio said what he did to warn us?"

A hope-filled smile spread across Isabelle's lips. "I believe that's exactly what he was doing. If he hadn't said what he did—if we'd have waited one more second to act—we might well be in Valli's hands right now."

Her words sent a chill up his spine. If they waited one more second to act, they might yet fall into Valli's hands. Levi closed his eyes for a moment and prayed, "Lord, may Sergio Cana not be punished for his bravery. And may we not waste his efforts." Then his eyelids snapped back open and he met Isabelle's eyes. "We need to get moving."

Dom Procopio rubbed his wrists where they'd been bound. "I will help you in any way I can. What is your plan?"

"We have to get the princess out of the country."

"That is wise," Dom agreed. "But judging from the number of soldiers who searched the cathedral earlier, I would guess that to be a very difficult task. Perhaps we should try to hide her inside the country."

"No." Isabelle inserted herself firmly in the discussion. "That would only give the insurgents greater opportunity to move forward with their plans. I *must* reestablish the rule of my family. I can't do that if I'm in hiding."

Levi placed a calming hand on her shoulder. "We'll get you out of this country." He turned to Dom. "We're less than two miles from the Sardis airport. Do you think you can get us there?"

"Get you to the airport?" Dom repeated, his round eyes thoughtful. "It might be possible, but you'd never get on a plane. Both of you would need passports, for one thing. And even if there were no soldiers at the airport, which would shock me, Her Highness is certain to be recognized."

The older man made many good points. Levi continued

to brainstorm. "The coast is just as close. Could you get us to a marina?"

"Do you have a boat?" Dom asked.

Levi shook his head regretfully.

"We could go through the mountains," Isabelle suggested.

Levi felt a jolt of fear at her suggestion. "We'd have to travel across the whole country. That's more than a hundred kilometers."

"And it's the last place they'd think to look."

Dom took her side. "There's a Sanctuary outpost on the Albanian border. You could cross there."

The same outpost where the fated message had been delivered by a man who ended up dead? Levi shook his head. "I don't know—"

"We'd still need passports to cross at the border and to make an international flight from Albania." Isabelle sighed. "My passport is back at the palace."

Levi reached inside a pocket on his bulletproof vest. "I have you covered there, Your Majesty." He held out his own passport and the fake passport Sanctuary had supplied him for the princess, which used an assumed name. "*If* we could get to the border—"

"I can get you to the border," Dom interrupted. "And I can get you across into Albania, no passport necessary. You can save that for your flight. The princess is far less likely to be recognized by Albanians than Lydians."

Unsure what the deacon meant, Levi looked into his round eyes. "You can get us into Albania without passports? How?"

"The Mursia River."

"All the bridges have border-crossing checkpoints."

"You're not going to use a bridge." Dom's smile was unsettling.

Levi opened his mouth to protest, but Isabelle cut him off. She'd been looking over his shoulder at the fake passport he'd provided. "This is a most unflattering picture of me."

"It was doctored," Levi explained, "to make you look less like a princess. The idea was to make you uglier because it hardly seemed possible to make you any prettier."

If Isabelle recognized his compliment as such, she didn't acknowledge it. "I look depressed. And bloated."

Dom peered at the picture. "You look nothing like yourself and yet just enough like yourself to pass for yourself. Sanctuary did a good job on this. It just might work."

The princess beamed at him. "Let's do it then. We need to hurry. Those soldiers could return at any moment." She turned her royal smile on Dom. "How are you going to get us to the river?"

While Levi struggled to think of how to talk Dom and Isabelle out of their crazy plan, the former Sanctuary agent outlined his strategy.

"The Cathedral Charity Store has a delivery truck. We often take excess donations across the border to ship to needy people in Eastern Europe, so it won't look out of place. Right now the back of the truck is filled with bags of donated clothing. The princess can hide among the bags." Dom looked at Levi. "As long as no one is looking for you, I suppose you can ride in the front with me."

"They'll recognize him," Isabelle explained. "The two of us went into the Embassy earlier. The security cameras surely got plenty of footage. If he's associated with me, we can't risk letting anyone see him."

"Fine. He can ride in the back of the truck, too." Dom switched off the television and headed out the door. "Let's get moving."

Shaking his head inwardly, Levi hurried to keep up. He could already imagine how his father would criticize the flaws in their absurd plan if his mission failed. Silently, he prayed God would help them out of a situation he feared was doomed from the start.

Isabelle nestled among the large plastic bags of donated clothing and prayed her hiding place wouldn't be discovered. She'd been in worse spots before, not even including what she'd experienced already that evening. How many times had she traveled to Africa with mission groups building deep water wells in remote villages? How many hospitals and schools had she visited in those tiny towns—and via far more rustic conditions than a truck filled with bags of clothing? At least she was warm and the bags of clothes were soft, cushioning the bumpy ride in a truck whose shocks, she realized, were shot. She made a mental note to donate a new delivery truck to the Cathedral Charity Store.

Assuming she survived long enough to do so.

"Are you doing all right?" Levi's voice carried clearly through the enclosed rear of the truck, in spite of the piles of bags that separated them.

"So far so good." She sighed, realizing how the attack and her flight from Lydia would change her plans. "I was supposed to be getting ready for a mission trip after the state dinner. I had originally planned to leave earlier this week, but then I would have missed the dinner. Now three African villages are going to have to wait for their deep water wells. Innocent children will continue to be exposed to deadly diseases from filthy water supplies. Do you think the insurgents thought of that before their attack?"

"I'm sorry," Levi apologized, though Isabelle knew it wasn't his fault. "You do a great deal of mission work overseas, don't you?"

"I feel it's my duty as a person of privilege. I'm in a unique position to not only raise the funds to improve people's lives, but also draw public attention to the plight of those in need."

Isabelle could picture the delighted faces of the children in the previous villages where she'd traveled to build wells. They'd been so jubilant when the water had started flowing. And the insurgent forces, by their rash act, had denied scores of children that happiness.

"I would like to promise you that we'll restore you to that position soon," Levi spoke with regret in his voice, "but I don't know what we're dealing with. Until we know who was behind today's attack, there will be little we can do to bring them to justice."

Isabelle sighed, the whole overwhelming situation more than she wanted to think about. Every time she considered the likelihood that her parents and siblings had died in the attack, she wanted to break down and cry. But there wasn't time to cry now. She had to focus on getting out alive. She owed that much to her family, whether they had lived or died, and to the children she hoped to someday help.

Trying to focus on the steps that would need to be taken before she'd be safe in the United States, Isabelle said, "I'd like to change into something more practical when we get to the border. Surely somewhere in these bags there are clothes that will fit me." Isabelle had made many donations of her own clothing to the charity shop, though she doubted any of it would make the trip in the truck. It usually sold quickly and at a premium price that helped fund the cathedral's charity work.

"Good idea," Levi agreed. "We don't know who might still be looking for us, even when we get to Albania. We want to avoid drawing attention to ourselves."

"You're exactly right. That's why I think you should shave off your beard."

When her suggestion was met with silence, Isabelle explained, "If Valli is affiliated with the insurgents, and if the Embassy security cameras have your picture, you need to do everything possible to avoid looking like you did when we stepped into the Embassy."

"Good point." Levi sighed. "And we need a cover."

"Cover?"

"Yes. An identity. It's not enough to simply try *not* to look like a princess and her bodyguard. We've got to be someone else—someone far removed from who we really are."

Isabelle realized his point was a good one. Once they were out of the Balkan region, perhaps she could get away without being recognized as the Lydian princess, but there were too many curious people-watchers in the world who would wonder what kind of business they were on. "We could be traveling students."

"That would work. I'm a little old for that, though."

"How old are you?" Isabelle realized she had no idea, having not thought about his age before.

"Thirty-one."

"Hmm." Yes, she had to admit it was a little old for pretending to be a student. "We need to be something far removed from who we really are," she repeated his instructions, trying to prompt her brain to think of possibilities. "How about poor people? Because I'm rich in real life, we could pretend to be poor people. I would match my passport photo then."

"Poor people making an international flight?"

She grumbled in her throat. What then? She tried to think of the people she'd seen in airports the many times she'd flown back and forth to the United States when she'd gone to college there. People traveling on business…but then they'd have to think of some business to be affiliated with. Too complicated.

Levi's suggestion about being far from who they were stuck in her mind. "The media have a distinct impression of who I am," she admitted slowly.

"I know." Levi's words were soft.

Her heart squeezed with shame and anger at Stephanos Valli and Tyrone Spiteri for causing the situation that had created her reputation. "Ever since my failed engagement the media had labeled me as someone who's unloving. Cold."

"The Ice Princess." Levi spoke the title gently, but his words still pierced her.

"I'm not like that." She shoved back a tear that had sneaked out. "How many orphans have I held? How many impoverished people have I embraced? I'm not unloving."

"But you haven't been romantically linked with anyone. And Tyrone's words after you broke off the engagement—"

She couldn't let him speak the words out loud. "*He* is the one who fooled *me*. Our engagement was nothing but a scheme for more power. He didn't care about me." The memories welled up despite her attempts to squash them. "Tyrone saw me as just another possession. He wanted to take me to make himself feel more powerful."

"Did he—" Levi began but then stopped. "I'm sorry. It's none of my business."

But Isabelle felt the need to set the record straight. In the darkness of the back of the truck, with Levi far removed from her by bags of clothing, she felt safe enough to admit out loud what she'd never told the press. "He tried to rape me," she spat the words out. "When he realized I'd seen through his facade, he knew I wouldn't go through with the wedding so he tried to force himself on me." She straightened with the one shred of dignity she'd saved. "But I fought him off."

"Good for you," Levi sounded sincerely proud of her. "How—"

"When I was in the United States in college there was a self-defense demonstration on campus. They showed us an eye-jab maneuver. I didn't get it exactly right, but I injured

Tyrone's right eye. He's nearly blind in it now—which I'm afraid only makes him hate me that much more."

"And that's why he maligned you to the media."

"Yes." Isabelle sighed. "He has them all convinced I'm too rigid to ever love a man. I suppose I could find a guy to have a fling with just to prove them all wrong, but that would be the wrong reason to start a relationship, and I won't do that to myself or some innocent man."

Levi was silent, and Isabelle wondered if she'd said too much. She hadn't talked about Tyrone in the two years since those events had taken place. She'd thought maybe she was getting over what had happened, but the vengeance she heard in her own words told her otherwise. Now she wished she hadn't spoken.

"Perhaps," Levi's voice carried quietly through the back of the truck, "we could use those impressions to our advantage."

It took Isabelle a moment to wrap her mind around what Levi was suggesting. "You mean, for our cover?"

"Yes. We could be a couple on a romantic getaway."

The moment Levi made his suggestion he feared he'd gone too far. Isabelle fell silent, and with regret he realized his idea likely only made her feel worse. He wasn't sure why she'd trusted him with the truth about what had happened to her. And now he'd betrayed that trust by proposing such a ridiculous idea.

"I don't—" she started, and Levi scrambled to think of some way to erase his suggestion.

But when she finished her sentence, he felt that much worse.

"I don't know how."

Levi's heart froze. "Your Majesty?"

"I'm sorry, Levi. It's a good idea. I just don't know if I

could pull it off. I haven't ever really dated—I was quite shel-
tered for so many years. My parents were so protective o
me I'd never really dated. Perhaps that's why I didn't realize
sooner what Tyrone was after and all the things that weren"
right about our engagement. I'm afraid I don't even know
how a person ought to act."

Her confession tore at him. No wonder she'd let the medi;
get away with calling her frigid. She didn't know *how* to
prove them wrong, and she was far too sensitive a soul to
flub up something so important.

"I shouldn't have suggested it," he apologized. "It sounded
like a good fit, but obviously…" He cleared his throat, unsure
when talking had become so difficult. "The student idea was
a good one. Perhaps we should just go with that."

He heard her sniffle from the other side of the bags of
clothes, and when she squeaked out, "Okay," he realized she
was having difficulty maintaining her composure.

His hand stretched across the bags in the darkness, and
he tentatively felt for her face. His fingers touched wetness
and he wiped away a stray tear before gently cupping her
cheek in his hand. To his surprise, instead of pulling away
she leaned her head toward his touch.

If it hadn't been for the bags between them he might have
pulled her into his arms. But then, he realized he ought to
be grateful their circumstances prevented him from getting
any closer to her. It would be so easy for him to forget tha
she was more than just a beautiful woman for whom he fel
growing affection. He couldn't lose sight of the fact that she
was royalty and likely the only surviving member of her
family. He'd promised King Philip he'd protect his daughter

And that meant keeping her safe from him, too.

With guilt, he wondered if he hadn't made the suggestion
of a romantic couple because of the growing affection he fel
for her. Was he subconsciously trying to get closer to her? He

had no right to feel the way he felt toward her. The sooner they could go their separate ways, the better off they'd both be.

Reluctantly he pulled his hand away from the warmth of her cheek. "It feels like the truck is slowing down. I wonder if we're nearing the border."

"The road has been curving quite a bit lately, which is typical of the mountain roads as we approach the border." Her voice held no more trace of emotion.

The truck eased around another corner and then slowed to a stop. Levi waited for Dom to open the rear door.

"If you'd like to find some clothes to change into, we can ask Dom if this is a good time."

"Okay."

A moment later the rear door of the truck cracked open and Dom's balding head was outlined by the moonlight. "We're at the Sanctuary outpost. I'm going to scope things out. You two stay out of sight for now." Then the door clicked shut and they were left in darkness again.

The minutes ticked by and soon Levi saw the greenish glow from Isabelle's phone.

"It's almost midnight," she whispered. "I hope Dom is okay."

"He's a professional," Levi reminded her, though he wondered how the aging man would fare if he encountered insurgents—and what the two of them would do if Dom ran into trouble.

A few moments later he heard the door to the cab of the truck open and the vehicle started again. His pulse kicked into high gear.

Isabelle whispered, "I hope that's Dom driving us."

"I hope so, too." The trucked rumbled over a bumpy stretch for what couldn't have been more than a few kilometers before coming to a stop again. In the stillness Levi could hear even footfalls as their driver came around to the back of the truck.

Levi reached for his sidearm and pulled it from its holster, aiming it at the door. Silently he turned off the safety and prayed.

FIVE

"Put down your gun, Levi," Dom said as he opened the rear door of the truck.

Relieved to hear the familiar voice, Levi engaged the safety and put his gun back in his holster. "How did you know I had my weapon drawn?"

"I'd be quite disappointed if you didn't. You're supposed to protect this little lady." Dom extended a hand to Isabelle as she waded over the bags in her evening gown. "Sorry for the excursion. Nothing appeared to be obviously amiss at the station, but I didn't recognize either of the men stationed there, and a still, small voice told me to get out of there. I've learned to listen when God talks to me."

"I appreciate that." Levi hopped out of the truck and looked back up the rutted path Dom had driven them down, which ran parallel to the Mursia River. He could just see the swirling waters beyond them in the moonlight. "Do you think anyone followed us?"

Dom blinked into the darkness. "If they did, they're awfully good at avoiding detection." He shivered visibly. "But I don't have a very good feeling about this. We need to hurry."

"May I please change clothes first?" the princess asked.

Dom agreed that Isabelle should find some clothes among the bags in the truck. He made sure she had a flashlight and then closed the door for privacy. Then he walked toward the river with Levi and spoke in a low voice. "Levi Grenaldo." He looked him in the eye. "I knew your father. We served together in this area years ago. He's a good man."

"Thank you." Levi cringed just a little at the comparison. His father's shoes would be difficult to fill, but he was determined to do his best.

Dom continued. "Because I trusted him, I will trust you. I honestly don't know how you're going to get Isabelle to the United States, but I will give you the best head start I can."

The ominous assessment did little to bolster Levi's courage. "I appreciate that."

"On the other side of the river there is a woodpile. Hidden in the middle, under quite a bit of wood and a tarp, is a motorcycle."

"Has it been started recently?" Given the age of the man he was speaking to, Levi feared the bike might be reduced to a pile of rust.

"Every couple of weeks, at least, the owner of the property on the other side gives the bike a go and makes sure it's filled with gas. But it belongs to Sanctuary, and I can't tell you how many refugees have traveled through this area on that bike."

"Where should I leave it when I'm done?"

"Park it at the airport. Someone will come along for it soon." Dom startled at a noise just downriver from them.

Levi spun around, pulling out his weapon.

"A raven." He lowered his gun as the bird took flight over the river.

"Ravens aren't active at night." Dom looked about warily. "Something startled that bird. You two had best get moving."

Levi rushed to the truck and knocked before opening the door. Isabelle had changed into a sloppy pair of oversize jeans with a bulky hooded sweatshirt. She looked less princesslike already. "We need to get moving."

"I can't find any shoes."

"Wear the ones you had on." Levi's sense of foreboding grew, and the hairs raised at the back of his neck as he listened to the vast darkness. "We need to hurry."

Isabelle slipped on the heeled leather pumps and clambered across the bags. She leaned toward him, and Levi caught her around the waist as she jumped down from the back of the truck. Too late he realized he wasn't prepared for such close contact with the princess. As she landed against him, she looked up and caught his eyes for just a moment.

His heart gave a lurch at the hopeful expression on her face. Did she really think he could get her to safety?

Could he?

She took a step back and he turned away. Too much still needed his attention. Joining Dom near the bank, Levi realized the older man held a crossbow.

"Perhaps you should shoot this." Dom held the heavy weapon toward Levi. "My eyesight isn't so good anymore, and you'll only get one chance to make a solid shot."

"What are you doing with that thing?" Isabelle asked as Levi took the cumbersome crossbow from Dom.

"There's a zip line attached to the bolt," Dom explained. "That's how you're going to get across the river."

Before Isabelle could react to Dom's explanation, Levi spun at the sound of rustling in nearby bushes.

All three of them looked in the direction of the sound. Levi could almost sense the presence of someone nearby, but in the darkness he could see no sign of anyone. The best he could do was hurry and get the princess across the river quickly. He'd hoped to change from his tuxedo before going any farther, but that issue seemed trivial compared to getting Isabelle safely out of Lydia.

"How does this work?" Levi looked over the bolt—the arrowlike projectile that would carry the zip line across the river. "Is there a pulley, or do we have to hold on with our bare hands?"

Dom reached across and touched a small steel bar. "It's a lightweight pulley. I'd recommend going one at a time. I'm not sure if it can hold you both." He pointed to a large tree across the river. "Try to sink the bolt solidly into that large tree."

Levi raised the crossbow and took aim. He didn't have much experience shooting crossbows, other than a brief orientation during his training with the Lydian military, but the tree was large and less than twenty meters away. And he had no other choice.

Just as he released the bolt a loud noise from behind startled him. He spun around, with no time to squint across the river in the darkness to determine if the bolt had hit his target. Two burly figures had jumped from the bushes along the riverside. One grabbed the princess from behind and appeared to be trying to carry her off, although her struggles hampered his efforts.

The second was locked in hand-to-hand combat with Dom. Levi hesitated only a second before slinging the zip line around the nearest tree branch and jamming the crossbow tight into the crook of the branch to secure it. Then he leapt at the man who was pulling the princess toward the bushes. Dom was a former agent. He would want Levi to attend to Isabelle's safety first.

Grabbing the muscular figure from behind, Levi attempted to wrench his thick arms away from Isabelle. He couldn't risk using his gun with the princess so entangled; instead he used two arms to pry away one of the hulking attacker's large fists.

Isabelle gasped and writhed but was no match for the

strong figure who held her. Desperately trying to think of a way to free her, Levi recalled that Isabelle had fought off Tyrone Spiteri by jabbing at his eyes.

It was the only decent idea he could think of. Clambering higher on the man's back, Levi reached around the attacker's head and dug at his eyes. With a furious yell, the assailant let go of the princess and grabbed Levi by the arms instead, throwing him over his back.

Levi spun in the air, for the first time in many years grateful for the gymnastics lessons his mother had enrolled him in as a child. He landed on his feet and darted after the princess, who'd dashed toward the river the moment the burly man had let go of her.

His only hope to outrun their oversize assailant, Levi barely caught sight of Dom still exchanging blows with the other attacker as he sprinted toward the tree that held the zip line. Scooping Isabelle around the waist with one arm as he ran, Levi grabbed the pulley where it was attached to the crossbow he'd jammed through the joint of the tree branch.

To his relief, the pulley disengaged just as their assailant hurled himself toward them. Levi pushed off with his feet, and he and the princess zipped along the taut wire across the gurgling waters of the Mursia.

Despite the relatively warm June weather they'd been experiencing, Levi knew the river was fed by the melting snow of the mountain streams and would likely be frigid. "Pull your feet up," he whispered to the princess, doing the same.

Unsure if the bolt he'd shot across the river had made solid purchase in the tree on the far side, Levi said a silent prayer that the lightweight pulley would hold them and that the grip of the line wouldn't fail.

The pulley groaned in his hand as the bank appeared just beyond them. "Lord, please don't let us fall," Levi whispered, just as he wondered how they might possibly land without crashing into the tree. The moment they reached the bank Levi let go of Isabelle, hoping she'd drop onto the soft earth before he braced himself for impact with the tree.

But to his surprise, Isabelle clung to his shoulders, extending her legs as they flew toward the tree. He kicked out with his feet.

They had no more than slammed into the tree when he let go of the pulley, simultaneously twisting around and trying to fall backward so he wouldn't crush the princess.

They came down in a tangle. Apparently Isabelle hadn't anticipated that he would let go so quickly because she still clung to him as though for dear life, her face pressed against his shoulder as they fell.

"Are you all right?" Levi whispered, wanting to attend to the princess but at the same time aware of the urgent necessity of cutting loose the zip line. Though they'd taken the only pulley across, the men could still easily use the line to reach them.

Clearly stunned by the fall, she panted audibly before whispering, "I'm fine. We should find cover, though. I can't imagine those goons will let us get away that easily."

Relieved that she hadn't been injured, he looked across the river and saw the first of their burly attackers making his way hand-over-hand along the zip line. He was nearly halfway across the river—and the second man wasn't far behind.

"Cover yourself," Levi instructed Isabelle, stepping in front of her as he pulled out his gun and shot the spot where the bolt was embedded in the tree. Splinters of wood exploded from the tree, exposing most of the bolt. Levi shot the spot again, standing clear as the bolt snapped free of the tree. With sharp cries, both of their attackers plunged into the frigid river. A moment later, all Levi could see was swirling water.

Unable to spot any sign of Dom on the other side, Levi risked calling out to him, "Are you all right, old friend?"

Dom's voice sounded weary. "A little worse for wear, but I'll be fine. The moment those two realized who was getting away, they lost interest in me."

"Glad to hear it! If you can get a message to the office in New York, let them know we're on our way. But be careful!"

"You're the ones who need to be careful." Dom's voice boomed back, stronger already. "Godspeed to you!"

"And to you!" Levi had spotted a wall of stacked split logs while he spoke to Dom. Pulling the princess up after him, he whispered, "This way!" and dashed toward where Dom had said the motorcycle could be found. He didn't know how many others might be right behind their two attackers. They'd have to move quickly.

Isabelle looked back at the Mursia River as Levi pulled her away from its banks. She tried to catch sight of the men who'd attacked them, but clouds had rolled in, obscuring even the pale light of the moon, and Isabelle could see nothing but the roiling waters. Had the men been swept downstream? Or were they even now crawling up the Albanian bank?

She turned her attention to Levi, who wrestled with something among the logs. "Can I help you?" She tried to catch her breath from her fight with the huge guy who'd jumped her. Fear chased up her spine, but she shivered it away, reassuring herself that Levi had been there. He'd rescued her from that awful man and his breath-crushing grip. Perhaps she could trust Levi—as much as she could trust anyone.

"I've got it," Levi whispered, pulling back a tarp before tugging on something that looked like handlebars.

"Is that a motorcycle?" Isabelle asked, blinking at the chrome just visible in the darkness.

"Yes." Levi threw aside an armful of logs, freeing the rear tire. "This is our ride to the airport."

Isabelle had been wondering how they would make the 250-kilometer trip to Albania's only international airport, which was nearly a four-hour drive from the Lydian border. She felt inside the waistband of her jeans to where she'd tucked her satin clutch, which held her cash and her phone. She didn't dare use her phone—there was too great a likelihood that the insurgent forces might be able to trace any calls she made. The longer she could stay off the radar, the better.

And the motorcycle looked like it would do the trick. "Do we have helmets?" she asked.

"Two." Levi unearthed them once he'd freed the bike, tapping the helmets together to shake out debris from the woodpile. "Now let's get moving. Those thugs who attacked us probably alerted others to our location before they jumped us. If they had confederates at the border station, they might cross into Albania and follow the highway looking for us—and that's the road we'll *have* to use to get to Tirana. Our only hope is to move faster than they do."

Nodding, Isabelle accepted the helmet and strapped it on. She didn't mind the idea of riding a motorcycle, but she sincerely wished she'd managed to secure more practical footwear. However, Levi was right. Their top priority was getting to the airport as quickly as possible. And maybe she would find a pair of boots or sneakers in one of the shops and boutiques inside the airport. She hadn't flown through the Albanian airport in a few years, but she recalled that it had enjoyable shopping.

Levi straddled the bike and patted the seat behind him.

With a gulp of courage, Isabelle hopped on the bike behind Levi. She had no more than tentatively wrapped her hands around his broad shoulders than he revved the engine and the bike moved forward.

They rumbled toward a rutted path in darkness.

"Perhaps you should turn on the headlight," she suggested.

"I don't want to give away our position."

"The engine noise does that." She found herself leaning close to his ear to be heard above its rumbling. "And we'll move faster if we can see where we're going."

"All right." Levi clicked on the light. "Pray this doesn't make us a target."

Isabelle pinched her eyes shut and prayed. The motorcycle picked up speed along the rutted road, and she could feel Levi shifting his weight from one side to the other to keep them from tipping on the uneven track. Hoping to help balance the bike, she focused on moving with him as he leaned to one side and then the other. The last thing they needed was to wipe out and injure themselves or damage the bike.

"Oh, Lord, get us out of here in one piece."

"What?" Levi's question made Isabelle realize she'd started praying out loud.

"Sorry. I was just praying."

"Well, keep it up. Here's the highway. Those guys' buddies could catch up to us anytime."

"Right." Isabelle peeked her eyes open just enough to see the paved track that wound its way up from the Mursia River through the mountains. Though she hated to think how easy they'd be to find on the highway, she knew of no other passable route through the jagged peaks. At least she'd gotten safely out of her own country. She could only hope the insurgents would move about less freely here.

With a smooth road stretching out before them, Levi picked up the bike's speed considerably. Isabelle relaxed now that she no longer had to worry about taking a spill on the rutted mountain path. She could feel exhaustion weighing on her, and realized she'd been up since six that morning. Though she wasn't about to attempt to pull out her phone to check the time, she knew it had to be well after midnight, and she was tired.

Gradually, as no one caught up to them and the road twisted endlessly before them, Isabelle's fears receded enough for her to contemplate the fix she was in. With her arms wrapped tight around Levi's shoulders and her body pressed to his, it was difficult not to think about the man who had done so much to secure her liberty.

She'd hadn't missed the compliment he'd paid her back in Dom's office—his comment that the Sanctuary agents had to make her picture uglier, since she couldn't be any prettier. Warmth spread through her at the memory of his kind words. Had he been trying to flirt with her? He didn't act flirtatious otherwise, but as she'd admitted to him already, she didn't have any experience with men. How would she know if he felt something for her? She felt her grip on his shoulders relax slightly as she pulled hesitantly away from him.

Levi nudged her with his elbow. "Don't fall asleep," he cautioned her. "I don't want you to fall off the bike."

Rather than let him believe she could possibly nod off with danger so close on their trail, Isabelle held on more securely, tucking her head against his broad back, out of the wind. Levi was a good man. And maybe she wouldn't mind if he felt something for her.

After her experiences with Tyrone Spiteri, she hadn't wanted anything to do with romance. But as she held tight to Levi's strong shoulders and their motorcycle hurtled through the mountains, she realized for the first time that she might not be so against falling in love, if she could fall in love with someone like Levi.

Deep darkness had settled over the landscape. As they approached Tirana, Albania's capital city, Isabelle wondered if she didn't see a hint of light in the east, or if it was simply the light of the city ahead of them. Rinas International Airport was located just northwest of the city, and they were approaching from the south, so they'd have to skirt the western edge of the metro area to get there.

Several headlights pierced the sky behind them. "Can you tell if we're being followed?" she asked Levi.

"No idea. Too many people are traveling into the city. The sun will be rising soon. I'll do what I can to keep ahead of whoever might be following us, but I don't want to draw too much attention to ourselves, either. As long as we're not attacked, I'll be happy."

Isabelle settled back as Levi followed the signs that pointed the way to the airport. When they arrived Levi found a place to park the bike, and Isabelle's legs wobbled unsteadily as she climbed off.

Immediately Levi's steady hand supported her back. He met her eyes. "You all right?"

"Just tired." She blinked back the sleep that had been creeping up on her all morning.

"You can sleep once we get on a plane. Until then, let's try to stick together." He discretely unbuckled a holster and gun, lifting the seat of the bike and depositing the weapon in the storage compartment. Isabelle realized it would do far more harm than good to attempt to bring the weapon inside, but she felt a twinge more vulnerable leaving it behind.

"Do me a favor." Levi reached toward her, plucking up the hood of her sweatshirt and settling it over her head. "Try to keep yourself covered as much as possible. I know this isn't your home country, but your picture is bound to have been on the news. Even if we've given the insurgents the slip, we can't risk anyone recognizing you. Not yet." He gently pulled the hood forward but didn't seem satisfied by what he'd accomplished. "Can you wear your hair down?"

"I never wear my hair down."

"Exactly. You're always pictured with it swept up. Even on

your mission trips you wear it up in a ponytail." His hands rested on the pins that held her upswept hair in place.

"Good point. You'll have to help me."

With the rising sun threatening to shed light on their actions, Isabelle worked quickly to pluck the pins from her hair, letting the disheveled curls fall past the sides of her face.

"Now we'll try the hood." Levi pushed her hair forward as he settled the hoodie atop her messy mane. "How's that?"

"Itchy."

He made a face, then pulled out his sunglasses and perched the oversize shades on her nose. A smile crinkled the corners of his eyes. "There. You hardly look like a princess."

Isabelle couldn't help smiling with relief that he'd managed to disguise her identity somewhat. "Itchiness is a small price to pay in exchange for anonymity. Now let's get rid of your beard so no one recognizes me because of you."

They entered the airport and immediately the bright lights and early-morning stream of passengers made Isabelle feel slightly better. Levi found the ticket desk and used his own credit card to buy tickets for the next available flight to New York City via Rome.

She breathed a sigh of relief once that important step was completed and they'd made it through security to the departure area, where many of the shops were located. They still had a couple of hours before the flight would board. "Let's get rid of that beard." She gave Levi's scruffy chin a pointed look. "And I'd like to get some more practical footwear, if that's at all possible."

They found sneakers in her size and comfortable socks to go with them. When Levi once again used his credit card to pay, all Isabelle could do was pray the insurgents hadn't matched his name to the face on the Embassy security camera—and she promised to pay him back as soon as she had the chance.

After grabbing a bite to eat, they picked up a shaving kit, but Levi balked when Isabelle suggested he leave her alone while he went into the men's room to shave.

"I'm not letting you out of my sight."

"What are you going to do—shave in a drinking fountain? Besides, I'd like to use the ladies' room before we board our flight." She watched Levi's eyes narrow slightly—a move she'd already come to associate with him digging in his heels.

He led her to a large map of the airport on a brightly lit central kiosk.

"There." He pointed to a mark on the map. "Family rest room."

She rolled her eyes at the stubborn man. "We're not a family."

"No—" he linked his arm through hers and led her in the direction of the restroom "—but it only has one door, so no one can walk in on you and carry you off. I'll stand guard outside."

Because there didn't appear to be any families waiting to use the special restroom at the early hour, Isabelle relented to allowing Levi to stand guard outside while she went in. After freshening up and brushing out the last of her royal hairdo, she stepped out. "Now it's your turn. I'll stand guard."

"You're not going to stand alone out in the open." Levi tugged her back inside the restroom. "You can wait in here while I shave."

Uncomfortable as she may have felt sharing the small room with him, Isabelle knew Levi had a point. And because he promised not to do anything more personal than shave off his beard, she figured it wasn't too inappropriate. As he'd pointed out several times already, she had a royal duty to stay safe. If that meant standing by while Levi shaved, it was a small price to pay.

Unsure if she ought to be looking at him, Isabelle could identify little else in the tiny room to keep her attention and found herself watching Levi as the white shaving foam he'd bought was peeled back by the razor, leaving a trail of tanned skin behind.

"You're not used to wearing a beard, are you?"

"No. Our fathers agreed it would be best if I disguised my appearance somewhat because I was a member of the Lydian army for four years and we weren't sure who might recognize me—good or bad."

"Our fathers?" Isabelle repeated.

"My father worked with yours to coordinate my position filling in for Alfred."

Having accepted Levi's hasty explanation for his role in protecting her back when they'd navigated the catacombs, Isabelle now realized she understood precious little about how he'd been appointed. "Why did they select you to guard me?"

Levi focused his eyes on his reflection in the mirror as he shaved and moved his mouth little as he explained, "None of the royal guard could be trusted. We had no way of knowing who else might be in league with the insurgents. When King Philip called the Sanctuary office, my father recognized that whoever was sent to protect you would need some level of familiarity with Lydia. Because I had spent so much time in the country, I was the obvious choice." He tapped his razor against the sink.

Piecing together the bits of the story he'd shared with her, Isabelle clarified, "So you're usually a bodyguard in the United States?"

Finished shaving, Levi turned on the water. "I'm not usually a bodyguard. I work for Sanctuary as a lawyer." He bent his head over the sink and splashed water on his face.

Isabelle studied the smudged white tuxedo shirt that stretched across Levi's well-muscled back as he washed the last of the shaving foam from his face. His jacket had never made it across the river. She pulled a few paper towels from the dispenser and handed them to him as he turned off the water.

"You're a lawyer?" The revelation made her consider how close she'd come to being captured so many times—and she hadn't even had a real bodyguard to protect her. "That's the best Sanctuary had? They couldn't even send a real body-guard?"

He lowered the paper towels from his face and his cold blue eyes met hers. For the first time she saw his whole face without the shaving foam and without the beard.

Oh, was he handsome!

Her heart gave a little flip as she saw—really saw—for the first time the man who'd saved her life so many times. With his face and neck bare of the dark hair, he suddenly seemed more human, and more vulnerable.

And, oh, was he mad!

He took a step closer to her in the tiny marble-tiled rest-room. "I got you safely out of the country, didn't I? How many thugs have I wrestled in the past twelve hours? How many times have I carried you?"

Isabelle swallowed and tried to look away, but his eyes held hers. She couldn't answer his questions—she'd lost count already. And she couldn't think straight with the sudden realization that had hit her.

She didn't want Levi to be upset with her. If they'd met under different circumstances, she could well imagine her-self having a crush on him.

Maybe she had a crush on him anyway.

But it was far too late to make a good first impression. "I'm sorry." She reached for his arm, but he stepped back beyond her reach. She let her hand fall to her side. "You've been an excellent bodyguard. I was just surprised. And I'm tired."

He turned his back to her and pitched the shaving items into the trash. "I'm tired, too. I shouldn't have snapped at you."

Isabelle studied his face in the mirror. He'd been plenty good-looking with the beard, she realized, but looking at him without it made her weak in the knees. She reached out a tentative hand and wiped away a bit of foam by his ear.

"You had a little shaving cream," she explained.

He met her eyes, and she felt her heart melt a little bit more. She cleared her throat. "I trust you." She looked at the door and wondered what they'd face once they stepped beyond it. "You're the only person I trust right now."

Levi didn't smile. "I can only pray that I will not fail your trust." He stepped between her and the door. "Because I'm only a lawyer."

SIX

Levi stepped cautiously from the restroom with Isabelle at his side. He studied the face of each person who passed by them, wondering how long it would be before their pursuers caught up to them and how he could possibly recognize them when they did. He didn't doubt that they would eventually track them to the airport. His only hope was to be ready when the next attack came.

To his relief, no one accosted them while they waited for their flight, and they were able to board the plane safely. Levi mentally cataloged each person near them on the plane, alert for the possibility that any of them might be trailing the princess. But no one seemed to pay them any extra attention. And no one seemed to recognize the princess among them.

Granted, Isabelle didn't look particularly royal in her cast-off jeans and bulky hooded sweatshirt. Her hair still obscured much of the sides of her face, and the only traces of makeup that remained from the evening before were the dark smudges under her eyes. She looked weary.

"Try to get some rest," he suggested as she settled in to the window seat and he took the place between her and the aisle. "Even if the insurgents know we're on this plane, I doubt they'll make any move until we land."

"That's what I'm afraid of," she whispered, leaning close

to his ear. "The men who were after us no doubt realize b
now that we made it into Albania, and if they guess that we'r
going to fly out, this is the only international airport. Do yo
think they'll realize we might be headed to New York?"

"It *is* the logical place for you to go. Even if they don'
realize the connection with Sanctuary, the United Nation
is headquartered in New York City, and we may need thei
help getting the insurgents removed. They may have alread
guessed that's where we're headed."

"So they may be waiting for us there."

Levi had reached the same conclusion already but appreci
ated that Isabelle had grasped the situation. At least he didn'
have to break the news to her. They weren't out of the wood
yet.

Far from it.

He could only imagine the insurgents would become mor
desperate the farther Isabelle flew from their clutches. H
was amazed the men at the river hadn't shot them on sight
but he wasn't about to mention that to the princess. She'
been through so much already.

Instead, he focused on easing her fears for their safety
"I'm the one they're least likely to recognize, especially no
that I've shaved off my beard. We'll stay on the plane when i
lands in Rome. I'll keep an eye out for trouble, but they ma
be waiting for us when we reach New York. When we exi
the plane, I'd like you to stay close behind me. If possible
keep your face blocked from view."

"How am I going to do that?" As they whispered, Isabell
had pulled her face closer to his. Now he could feel her breath
near his ear as she spoke and caught the sweet scent of th
cinnamon roll she'd eaten at the airport.

Refusing to be distracted, he focused on the challenge
ahead of them. "Keep your hair down and your hood up. Tha

hould help. Wear my sunglasses and walk close to me. Bury our face against my shoulder as much as you can."

"I thought we were going to try to act like students," Isbelle challenged him. "This sounds more like your other lan."

"For this purpose, acting like we're a couple may be more ractical. Just hold my hand and try to keep your face out of ight." He dipped his head so he could see her eyes clearly nd was surprised by how close their faces were in the tight uarters of the coach-class seats. His breath caught. "Can ou handle that?"

Her warm brown eyes looked hesitant, but then a smile ent her lips. "It's too late to buy a burqa, so I guess your lan will have to work."

The smile warmed him far more than it should have, and e found himself smiling back. It occurred to him that he vouldn't have to fake anything to play a man in love with her. he real trick would be convincing himself that he felt nothng. "Good. Don't worry about our landing. Get some rest."

Their flight to Rome would last just over an hour—they vouldn't even change time zones—and Levi was determined o let Isabelle get as much sleep as possible. Although he vas exhausted, he couldn't risk sleeping through their stop n Rome. Once they were back in the air again he'd rest on he flight to New York—assuming they made it that far.

To his relief, Isabelle slept through their stop, which was neventful. Once the plane was in the air again, he settled n to rest. It was a ten-hour flight to New York, but with the ix-hour difference in time zones, it would only be four hours ater when they landed—just before noon if everything went moothly. And Levi prayed everything would go smoothly.

Isabelle awoke somewhere over the Atlantic Ocean with a ink in her neck. Levi slept soundly with his head lolled back in his seat. She marveled that he could still look so handsome in such an awkward position.

A small plastic cup of liquid was perched on the tray from of her. Recognizing her in-flight Coke, she downed the drink grateful for something to wet her throat after the dry air of the plane and hoping the caffeine would help her wake up.

The sunrise had caught up with them and now bright light streamed in through the cabin windows. Isabelle would have been surprised that Levi could sleep in the circumstances except that she knew he had to be exhausted. She had been too.

So much had happened since the last time she'd slept. The day of the state dinner had been a busy one, and she'd had just enough time to get ready and dash to her limousine before her entire world had been rocked by the blasts from the ambush. Her life now felt like the images she'd seen on Dom's television of the burned-out remnants of the royal mo torcade: a smoking, hollow shell of what it once had been.

She thought back to that newscast and the absence of any bodies among the wreckage of the royal motorcade. Her father had been wise to keep her siblings separated. Was it possible her brother or sister had survived the attack? Isabelle recalled the way the hood of a vehicle had slammed into the windshield of her car. Could anyone have survived such a blast? Or might her brother have escaped before the explo sion?

She could only be certain of one thing—she was alive. And as long as she was alive, for however long it took, she'd do what she could to bring the insurgent forces to justice. I any members of her family had lived long enough to escape she prayed God would be with them and keep them safe.

As Isabelle's prayers for her family poured from her heart silently to God, the plane ride passed quickly. Soon she could see the Statue of Liberty welcoming them as she had many weary traveler over the years. New York spread out beyond them as the plane neared JFK airport.

Because Levi looked so peaceful in his sleep, Isabelle was reluctant to wake him. When she finally nudged him awake as the plane prepared to land, she realized with regret that they didn't have much time to discuss where they were headed once they left the airport. She knew he planned to take her to Sanctuary International headquarters, but she had no idea where that was, other than being somewhere in the vast city.

As soon as his eyes popped open, Levi appeared to be in bodyguard mode again. "I'm going to call someone to pick us up," he explained quietly as he straightened from his slumped sleeping position. "But we'll have to be careful. We don't want to lead anyone back to the Sanctuary headquarters. The headquarters are disguised and unlisted. We can't risk giving away their location—for your safety and that of so many others. If I have any concerns that we're being followed, we'll take a circuitous route and switch cars if we have to."

"What if we become separated?" Isabelle had never had to navigate the city or its complicated transportation systems alone—and now was the worst possible time to have to learn.

Levi looked almost startled by her question. "You're going to stick so close beside me that no one can see your face," he reminded her.

"But if we have to switch cars—"

"Then go to the UN." He stood as the passengers rose to exit the plane.

Isabelle rose next to him and fluffed out her hair to hide as much of the sides of her face as possible before slipping on the sunglasses.

Then Levi wrapped his arm around her back and pulled her close against his shoulder. "Let's stay in the middle of the crush of exiting passengers. That will help obscure us. And you need to keep your head down. I'll keep an eye out for trouble."

Isabelle obediently ducked her head against his shoulder, pressing her cheek against the smooth cotton of his shirt. She could feel his pulse beating away with a steady, reassuring rhythm as they paused in line, waiting to leave the plane.

Her own pulse had kicked into an anxious staccato as she tried to anticipate what might be waiting for them. Much as she wanted to believe that they were almost to safety, she'd thought the same thing when they'd entered the Embassy in Sardis. And she'd been so very wrong then.

As they stepped into the airport the crowd shifted, and their fellow passengers dispersed. Although she'd flown into JFK more than once over the years, Isabelle hardly knew her way around the vast complex of gates. She kept her eyes on the floor and focused on matching Levi's stride as he made his way through the terminal, trusting him to find the way and avoid trouble.

The muscles in his shoulder tensed.

"What?" she whispered.

"I'm not sure—" he kept moving and didn't look down "—so many people are moving in the same direction, it's difficult to tell if any of them are following us."

Isabelle didn't know what to make of his comment, but she took it as a bad sign. She doubted Levi would have admitted his concern if he hadn't sincerely suspected someone was showing them undue interest. But there was little she could do other than keep her head down and keep moving.

She let herself breathe a small sigh of relief once Levi had completed his phone call to the Sanctuary office for a ride. "How are we doing?" she asked, keeping her face in his shadow as she looked up in an attempt to read his expression.

The slight smile on his lips was warm, but his eyes looked

wary. "We're going to have to play the couple," he said, leaning down to nuzzle her forehead with his nose.

The contact surprised her, but she also found it comforting and had to remind herself that he was only acting. She leaned into him slightly. "You think we're being followed?"

His nose traced her hairline until his lips hovered just beyond her ear. "There are two men who've been behind us ever since we left the plane. One of them took your picture a moment ago, though I can't imagine he got much more than your hair."

Isabelle's breath caught and she rested her forehead against Levi, needing the comfort his presence offered, even if they weren't really the couple they wanted everyone else to see. As a member of the royal family, she'd had her picture snapped by strangers many times—but none of those strangers had been out to kill her.

"What are we going to do?" she asked quietly, aware that the man she spoke to wasn't a bodyguard or even a Sanctuary International agent. He was a lawyer, and for all she knew he didn't have any clue more than she did about evading the men who were after her.

But she didn't have anyone else to turn to.

"We'll have to kill time before the car arrives. I'm going to try to shake them. Whatever you do, stay close to me and keep your face out of sight. As long as they're not sure you're the person they're supposed to be following, we stand a chance of losing them."

Isabelle did exactly as she was told, keeping her face out of sight and hoping she and Levi looked like a romantic couple. They paused several times with Levi's arms around her, his face close to hers as they consulted about their next move, hoping to give anyone watching them the impression that they were two people in love, so absorbed with one another that they didn't care about anything beyond themselves. Their cover was so far from the truth—and yet Isabelle found herself wanting to believe it, to feel the affection Levi offered as he pressed his lips near her ear, to believe that the arms around her were not a shield, but a loving embrace.

"Now what?" Isabelle asked as they came to a stop near the doors to the outside.

"Here comes our car," Levi sounded hesitant, "right on time."

"Are we going to get in it?"

"Those two men are still watching us."

Isabelle's heart sunk. After all their maneuvering she couldn't imagine the men were following them by accident. She wrapped both arms around Levi's shoulders, wishing there was some way she could hide. But obviously they'd already found her. She hiccupped back a fearful sob.

Levi's arms wrapped around her, pulling her closer into his warm embrace.

"Do something," she begged him, daring to look up into his eyes.

He bent his face closer to hers and his lips grazed the arch of one eyebrow.

Isabelle recalled all the negative articles that had followed her breakup with Tyrone Spiteri. They'd called her frigid, dispassionate, unloving. But she was none of those things.

Tentatively, she raised her face closer to his.

The men were searching for the Ice Princess. They didn't think she was capable of affection. Could she throw them off her trail?

Levi cupped her face in both hands, as though he could block all sight of her from the men who were watching. "Shall I?" he asked hesitantly, drawing closer by millimeters.

Instantly she realized what he was about to do. At the same second, she knew she sincerely wanted him to.

Unable to find her voice, Isabelle gave a tiny nod, and then Levi's lips met hers.

It was nothing like the kisses she'd shared with Tyrone—*nothing* like them. Relief washed over her along with a rush of attraction toward the man who'd proved she really was capable of affection.

No matter what the media said.

Her hands tightened their grip on his shoulders and she rose up on her tiptoes as though doing so would help her kiss him better. To her delight, he didn't pull away but seemed to lose himself in the contact between them.

Lightheaded, Isabelle pulled back just long enough to catch a breath.

"They've turned away." Levi's words jolted her back to reality. "Now." He slipped one hand into hers and tugged her toward the car.

They were moving away from the station by the time Isabelle collected her thoughts. "Did they follow us?" she asked, still trying to straighten her head out after that mind-blowing encounter.

"No. I saw them looking back inside the airport as we pulled away—they're well out of sight now." He pulled back from her for the first time since they'd left the plane. "You can stop hiding for now."

"Thank you." She turned away from him and watched New York slipping by out the window. It would be wise, she knew, to keep her distance from Levi as much as possible. His kiss had only been meant to throw off her pursuers. In her head she knew that. Now if only she could convince her heart, which was leaping about inside her and couldn't seem to understand why she was no longer in his arms.

Meanwhile, Levi was on his phone talking in low tones and consulting with their driver. She quickly determined there was no point trying to sort out what was going on by listening to his half of the conversation. She'd leave that to him while she sorted through the crashing waves of emotion that assaulted her heart.

Levi's tug on her hand a little later pulled her out of her thoughts.

"Are we there?"

"No." Levi cleared his throat. "We're at Central Park. We're going to hop out and walk a few blocks while the car circles back again. If we decide the coast is clear, we'll get back in the car."

Isabelle didn't have to ask if he thought they were being followed again. She doubted he'd risk taking her out in the open if he didn't feel it was necessary. "And what if the coast isn't clear?"

"It's a big park."

"Levi?"

"We'll try to hide. I've got my phone. If I need to, I can ask Sanctuary to send out decoy princesses, but I don't want it to come to that."

"Why not?"

"Right now there's still a chance they aren't sure they're following the right person. If we send out decoys, they'll know you're in the city." He reached for the door handle. "Ready?"

"I guess."

They stepped out of the car and Levi pulled her into his arms again as they stepped onto the sidewalk. "As a precautionary measure, you should probably still keep your face out of sight. We don't need anyone recognizing you—no matter who they are. By now I'm sure the international news has reported the attack on your family. People everywhere will have seen your picture on their televisions. If they see you walking around their city, there's bound to be a fuss."

"We don't need a fuss," Isabelle agreed, keeping her face

turned toward his shoulder, although his closeness was too fresh a reminder of the fantastic kiss they'd shared. But she was determined to follow his instructions until they'd reached safety. Then she could worry about keeping her distance from him.

Levi set a leisurely pace, stopping now and then to pull her into his arms, though she knew he was looking past her, not looking at her. She feared at any moment someone would leap out from behind a tree, but after some time, Levi surprised her by saying, "Here comes the car again."

"Is the coast clear?"

"I guess we'll find out." He tugged her back to the vehicle and they slipped quickly inside.

They drove around for a few more minutes before Levi leaned back from conversing with their driver. "This may be our best chance." He scooped up her hand and met her eyes.

"Chance?"

"We're getting out a few blocks from headquarters. I don't want to risk leading them there, but I think—" he cast a glance through the back window "—I think we'll be okay." He opened the door and they stepped out onto a bustling sidewalk.

With her face turned toward Levi and her eyes on her feet, Isabelle wasn't even sure which part of the city they were walking through, but she stuck close to Levi and trusted him to get her to Sanctuary. As they crossed one street and then another, her hopes rose that they were going to make it to safety after all.

When they turned down an alley, Isabelle wanted to ask Levi where he was headed, but he quickly picked up his pace and, a moment later, broke into a run.

As Isabelle ran beside him she felt even more grateful that she'd been able to buy a pair of sneakers. She could hear footsteps pounding the pavement behind them. They had to get away! She tried to sprint faster. Seconds later a large figure jumped Levi from behind and he went down.

Thick arms wrapped around her, lifting her off her feet. She caught a glimpse of Levi struggling with two attackers as the thug who held her spun her around, carrying her quickly back up the alley the way they'd come.

Whipping her arm back, Isabelle managed to catch the brute in the nose with a hard jab from her elbow. His steps faltered as blood poured from his nostrils, but he kept moving.

Kicking at his legs as he carried her, Isabelle attempted to knock the man's feet out from under him. She could see a car running up ahead, parked at the entrance to the alleyway, its windows tinted just dark enough that she couldn't make out who waited inside.

She couldn't let the man get her inside that car!

Jabbing her feet toward his legs with desperate strength, Isabelle finally caught the man square on one knee. The joint buckled and he sagged toward the ground. She whipped back with her elbow again, this time catching him full in the face and sending his head snapping back with a grunt.

His grip loosened slightly and she flung herself from his arms, spinning around and tearing back down the alley toward where Levi was fighting off two other large men. With her loose hair streaming past her eyes she couldn't see much, but she ran toward him with everything in her, hoping to jump the attacker nearest her as soon as she reached him.

Footsteps tore up the alley behind her. She was nearly to Levi when a fresh set of arms plucked her up. She could immediately tell the man who held her was smaller than the one who'd carried her off the first time. He must have come from the waiting car.

Isabelle tried the elbow trick again but the man ducked, avoiding the blow. She extended her arm and managed to free her hand from his grasp. This smaller guy wasn't able to carry her nearly as swiftly as the first thug.

Swinging toward his face with her free hand, Isabelle managed to knock him in the ear. It must have stunned him because his progress up the alley wavered. She tried the move again and he lost more speed. Pulling back her arm for another blow, she hoped to free herself from his grasp in another moment.

She hardly heard the footsteps rushing up behind her until the moment before she felt the other man leap upon them.

SEVEN

Levi's head swam from the blows he'd taken, but he couldn't let that slow him down. He launched himself at the man who struggled with the princess, peeling him away from her just enough to allow him to get in a good slug at the attacker's jaw.

The man wavered in midair a moment. Levi caught him with an uppercut punch under the ribs and he seemed to deflate backward. Spinning around to face Isabelle, Levi was horrified to see her covered in blood. "Are you all right?"

She opened her mouth as though to respond, but at that very moment a large figure staggered toward them, bleeding profusely from his nose. The lumbering brute was enormous. Levi fought back the darkness that seemed intent on invading his line of sight. His struggle with the other men had left him on the verge of passing out. But he knew that if he lost consciousness, Isabelle would undoubtedly be captured.

Mustering what strength he had left, Levi thrust his leg out in a high round kick and caught the thug near his ear. The man shook off the blow and reared toward him. Levi scuttled backward, wishing he had some weapon to use. Instead the best he could do was evade the oncoming attack.

The man came at him swinging and Levi ducked, avoiding the first blow but taking the second in a grazing shot along his jaw. Light exploded behind his eyes, but Levi blinked it back, shuffling out of the way as the man lunged at him again. He was aware of the princess just behind him.

"Run!" he told her, hoping this last attacker was the only one who remained.

"I don't know where—" she began to protest.

But Levi shook his head as he ducked away from another swinging fist. He held out his arms and continued backward, trying to block the bleeding man from reaching Isabelle. "Just get away. Anywhere."

The swinging fists picked up speed. Levi ducked back again and again before the attacker caught him in a solid punch to his gut.

Air whooshed from his lungs and the sky spun.

He heard Isabelle scream, and as he blinked back the blood that ran from a cut on his eyebrow, he saw the princess swinging something at their attacker's head. When he saw the man go down, Levi sagged forward in relief.

Isabelle stepped under his arm, and he slumped against her. "Stay with me, Levi," she whispered, patting his cheek. "Tell me how to get to Sanctuary before any more of those guys show up."

Stars danced behind his eyes, and Levi knew he was leaning heavily on the princess, but it was all he could do to stay conscious. When he spoke, his lips felt swollen and unfamiliar, and he realized the men who'd assaulted them had gotten in several hard blows to his face. "Down this alley. Two blocks. Don't let them—" he gulped a steadying breath "—see where we go."

"All right." Isabelle hoisted him a little higher and tucked one arm more securely around his waist. "Can you walk at all?"

Levi was able to get his legs moving, but the action seemed to demand as much from his system as he could possibly handle. After several steps blackness and stars clouded his vision, and he paused. "I'm sorry," he panted between breaths.

"It's all right."

"No." He wanted to look behind them to see if any of their attackers had roused, but turning his head only brought on another onslaught of stars, and his field of vision blurred completely. "Can you see the men behind us?"

Isabelle looked back for him. "They haven't moved."

Relieved to hear it, Levi nonetheless knew the men could regain consciousness and come after them at any moment. He couldn't let the princess be captured. Pressing on, he told Isabelle, "We'll come to a door on the right side of the alley that says *Sanctuary* in small blue letters. It's in the middle of the block. The pass code is eleven, sixteen, seventeen." His words came out between gulping breaths. "If the men come after us, drop me and run for that door."

"I'm not going to leave you," Isabelle protested.

Levi stopped on his tracks. He had to make her understand. "You will leave me," he said, fixing his eyes on hers. "It is your royal duty. You cannot endanger yourself for me. If those men capture you, I fear the Royal House of Lydia will end."

Isabelle absorbed his message with a solemn expression. Then she glanced back. "They still haven't budged. Come on. If we hurry, getting captured won't be an issue."

She propped him up a little straighter and moved forward, faster this time.

When his steps slowed, she all but pulled him. "Lean on me, Levi," she whispered. "We're getting there."

His closed his eyes and focused on matching her steps. When he faltered, she encouraged him, "Half a block more. I'll drag you if I have to."

The sky seemed to tilt and sway, and the next thing he

knew, she had him propped against the doorway as she entered the numbers he'd given her. It seemed to take all his strength to make the step over the threshold. As the darkness closed in, he forced himself to fall forward so that he wouldn't block Isabelle from closing the door securely behind him.

Isabelle daubed gently at the wounds on Levi's face. She was certain the cut on his eyebrow could use stitches, but after the men who'd helped her carry him to the couch had found a first aid kit for her, they'd apologized about not being able to help more. There was a crisis somewhere, and everyone in the Sanctuary office was upstairs trying to resolve the issue. It occurred to Isabelle after the men left that *she* might be the very issue everyone was trying to resolve, but by the time that thought occurred to her, the men were gone.

She and Levi were on their own.

At least she was able to clean Levi's wounds and wash the blood from her hair in the nearby kitchenette. It saddened her, what those horrible thugs had done to Levi, leaving his handsome face swollen and bruised. After she'd bandaged up the worst of his injuries, she cupped his cheek in her hand, surveying the damage and trying to determine what else she might be able to do to help him.

After all, he'd done so much to help her.

Moments later, she felt his head shift in her hand, and Levi showed signs of rousing.

She couldn't help smiling down at him as his eyelids fluttered open. "I was afraid I was going to have to take you to a hospital," she chided him.

"Where are we?" He blinked several times.

"The back lobby of Sanctuary. At least I think that's where we are. Anyway, I entered those numbers at the door you told me to find, and it opened."

Levi's eyes seemed to come into focus. "Yes, this is the back lobby. You did an excellent job getting me here."

"I wouldn't have made it much farther." She closed up the first aid kit and gathered up the empty packets of ointment. Because he'd finally awakened, she wanted to keep him talking to help him stay conscious. "What were the numbers anyway?" she asked as she headed to a nearby wastebasket.

"Hmm?"

"The pass code for the door. Is that a Bible verse?"

"Ah." Recognition filtered across his face. "Ezekiel 11:16 and 17. 'The Lord says: Although I sent them far away among the nations and scattered them among the countries, yet for a little while I have been a sanctuary for them in the countries where they have gone. I will gather you from the nations and bring you back from the countries where you have been scattered, and I will give you back the land again.'" As he quoted the verses, his voice strengthened.

Isabelle felt a chill chase up her spine as Levi spoke the ancient words. "'I will bring you back.'" She repeated God's promise softly, kneeling on the floor beside the couch where he rested. "'I will give you the land again.'"

"Those verses are part of the Mission Statement of Sanctuary International." Levi turned his head slowly toward her. "God was a sanctuary for the children of Israel. And we try to help people find sanctuary today, with the hope that someday some of them might be able to return to their homeland."

"I'd like to return to Lydia." Isabelle cleared her throat. "I'd like Lydia to be returned to my family."

As she spoke, voices echoed down the hall, and moments later several figures entered the room. One of the men who'd helped her get Levi to the couch led the way, explaining, "I didn't think to ask who they were. How was I supposed to recognize them covered in blood?"

As he spoke, a handful of men surrounded them, and a

silver-haired man extended his hand. "Princess Isabelle?" he asked.

"Yes." She rose and shook his hand, warmed by his use of her title, in spite of her fear that it might no longer apply if the insurgents had taken over her government.

"I'm Nicolas Grenaldo, president of Sanctuary International. On behalf of our organization I'd like to welcome you and thank you for rescuing my son." He looked down at where Levi lay on the sofa. "He was supposed to be rescuing you."

Isabelle looked quickly back and forth between father and son, putting together the missing pieces. Levi hadn't told her that his father was the *president* of Sanctuary International. Even as she absorbed that news, she hurried to set the record straight. "Thank you for your kind words of welcome. I'm afraid I did very little to get us here. Levi fought off many assailants and carried me more times than I can count. We were nearly overcome in the alley when I was lucky enough to find a length of steel pipe to knock out the man who tried to kidnap me. Other than that little bit of effort, all the credit goes to your son that I'm alive at all."

Through the weary lines that had engraved themselves on his face, Nicolas Grenaldo beamed at her. "Praise the Lord for that length of steel pipe then and for your escape from those who would have harmed you. Our office has been turned upside down by the events of the past day, and we're making every effort to determine the fate of the rest of your family."

At his mention of her missing family members, Isabelle felt her heart catch, and her hands began to tremble. "Please, sir, do you know what has become of them?" She braced herself for the news. She'd been resigning herself to a grim outcome ever since she'd seen the first fiery blast sear the sky, but now she felt as though the gavel hung suspended in the air, ready to drop.

Sympathy filled the man's face, and Isabelle feared for the worst.

"You are the first member of the royal family to be recovered. We have no evidence to support the insurgent claims that your entire family is dead. There have been no bodies identified as members of the royal family. Our agents in Lydia have confirmed that none of those killed in the attacks fit the description of any member of the royal family. Indeed, the three dead have all passed preliminary identification. They were two drivers and a guard."

"Three bodies?" Isabelle heard her voice speaking, but she felt as though she was watching the conversation from somewhere else. No doubt, even if they weren't her family members, the drivers and guard would have been people she'd known. She grieved that they'd died so needlessly.

The man who'd stood by Nicolas's side now spoke up. "We believe that if the insurgent forces had any proof any member of the royal family had been killed, they would have made that news public knowledge. Moreover, they would have touted that as evidence of their victory. They have nothing to gain from hiding that fact, if it were true, and everything to lose."

"So my family may still be alive?"

Nicolas Grenaldo placed his hand on her shoulder. "We pray they are alive. More than that, we pray for their safety. You have overcome many obstacles in your efforts to reach us. The fact that the other members of your family have not yet made public the news of their survival means they likely are in no position to make their whereabouts known."

Isabelle struggled to untangle the meaning of his words from the decorum with which he'd spoken. "They're in danger," she realized aloud. "Likely greater danger than we have already faced."

Nicolas nodded solemnly. "We must continue to pursue every avenue for their rescue. But now, I must report the good news of your survival—"

Before the Sanctuary president could continue, Levi sat up straighter and interrupted him. "No. Don't let anyone know she's alive."

"What?" Father stared down at son in disbelief.

The act of sitting up must have been nearly too much for Levi because he wavered unsteadily before speaking. "We believe the American ambassador to Lydia, Stephanos Valli, may be in league with the insurgents."

Nicolas's face clouded. "That would be most unfortunate. We've been freely sharing information with his office."

"Stop sharing," Levi ordered, his tone much stronger now. "We cannot risk giving away anything. Not yet. Not until we know we can keep Her Majesty safe."

Isabelle felt grateful for Levi's defense. She didn't want Stephanos Valli to know where she was—even if he already knew she was alive.

As she watched, Nicolas Grenaldo narrowed his eyes, and his balding head turned red. She could tell he was upset— whether with Levi or Stephanos, she wasn't sure. But his expression was forcibly pleasant when he turned to her.

"I'm sure you'll want to freshen up, Your Majesty. Levi will need to update our team. Samantha can take care of your needs now." Nicolas stepped back, and a youngish blonde woman led Isabelle down the hall.

"Right this way."

Levi watched Samantha Klein lead Isabelle down the hall, and his gut churned. Samantha didn't like him—not since he'd rejected her advances toward him a couple of years before. What if she conveyed her distaste for him to Isabelle? His father had already displayed a marked lack of esteem for his skills. What would Isabelle think of him?

He tried to convince himself it didn't matter what Isabelle thought about him—that he had played his role in her rescue and might never even see her again. But his heart refused to believe it.

"Levi—" his father turned and led the men away, calling back to him as he left "—clean up and meet me in the third floor conference room in twenty minutes. I need your intel, and I need it yesterday."

"I'll be right there." Levi stood on shaking legs and tried not to pass out. He had a bathroom with a shower off his office and a selection of clothes there. Other than his old room at his parents' house, it was the closest thing to a home he had. It was all the home he'd needed since he'd finished law school and spent all his time working.

He slumped against the railing in the elevator and made it to his office without passing out. Catching a glimpse of his reflection in the mirror, he cringed. His face was a patch-work of cuts and bruises, and blood continued to seep from the butterfly bandage Isabelle had stuck to his eyebrow.

Turning away from the mirror, he cleaned off and changed clothes. Despite of his best efforts, he arrived at the conference room twenty-three minutes after his father had left him. He was three minutes late—a fact his father would undoubtedly take note of and not forget.

"We've pulled up the file on Stephanos Valli." Nicolas shot Levi a look as he entered, communicating with certainty that he was aware of every second they'd waited. "He was born Steven Valli in Elmhurst, Pennsylvania, in 1953. His maternal grandfather had immigrated to the United States from Lydia, and his grandmother was of Greek descent. A perfect fit for the Lydian ambassador, between his Ivy League education and his pedigree. He even changed his name to Stephanos when he was appointed ambassador to Lydia to make himself more relatable to the Lydian people. So what makes you think he's in league with the insurgents? What would he possibly have to gain when he clearly would have so much to lose?"

"I tried to take Isabelle to Valli after the ambush." Levi placed both hands on the conference table, as much to prop himself upright as to make eye contact with his father across the table. He realized much of his negative impression of Valli was based on Isabelle's repugnance toward the man. But they had facts on their side, too. "When we entered the Embassy there were Lydian soldiers standing guard. Two of them tried to take our weapons. A third, whom the princess identified as being a friend of her brother, Alexander, made a statement that Isabelle felt was intended to warn us away from Valli."

"What did the soldier say?"

Levi did his best to quote the man verbatim. "He said, 'Oh good, you've captured the princess. Valli will be so pleased.'"

"Captured?" Nicolas Grenaldo breathed the word with incredulity in his tone. "Why would Valli want to capture the princess?"

"Why would anyone want to destroy the royal family?" Levi met his father's eyes. "The nation of Lydia is a small, peaceable country with little economic impact and no known enemies. What would anyone have to gain?"

The sound of a throat clearing behind him sent Levi spinning around.

Isabelle entered the room. She wore khaki slacks and a simple navy button-down blouse, and her still-damp hair hung in drying curls down her back.

The sight of her took Levi's breath away. "Your Majesty." His throat was suddenly dry.

The princess must have heard the last of their conversation because she jumped right in. "Stephanos Valli has tried to manipulate my family for his own benefit before. He convinced my father to initiate a marriage contract between me and Greek businessman Tyrone Spiteri. When that agreement ended, Valli made it very clear where his allegiances lay."

Nicolas nodded. "Valli criticized the royal family for ending the engagement."

"Yes." A touch of color rose to Isabelle's cheeks. "He publically maligned me and tried to undermine the authority of my father's rule. Were it not for my father's affection for the United States and his connection to this country through my mother, he would have had Valli removed from Lydia."

The Sanctuary president absorbed the information. "We don't know why the royal family was ambushed. No one has stepped forward to claim responsibility for the attacks. It's possible Valli might be involved." His silvery eyes roved the room. "But you said *Lydian* soldiers were guarding the Embassy. The king is the head of the army. Who told them to capture the princess?"

Isabelle shook her head thoughtfully. "Three generals serve under my father. I am on familiar terms with David Bardici, Corban Lucca and Marc Petrela. I hate to think they would conspire against the royal family."

"I hate to think anyone would do this," Nicolas Grenaldo commiserated, "but someone did, and your generals have done nothing to stop it. Corban Lucca was in the motorcade at the time of the ambush. He has not been heard from since. We've been in contact with Bardici and Petrela, but neither of them have said anything to indicate any animosity toward the crown or involvement with the insurgents."

"Someone has to be working with Valli." Levi wouldn't let them lose sight of the facts. "Host country officials are not allowed to enter a representing country's embassy without permission. Yet those Lydian soldiers appeared to be stationed there and answering to Valli. That tells us there is a conspiracy at work here, and Valli *must* be in on it."

Isabelle nodded her agreement. "What about the prime minister? Have you been in contact with Gloria Emini?"

"Prime Minister Emini has Parliament at the ready to host a special session as soon as need arises, but she cannot hold an official session without the consent of the ruling sovereign." Nicolas gave Isabelle a pointed look. "Her biggest concern is locating the Head of State or, in the king's absence, crowning a successor."

Isabelle's face blanched noticeably.

Levi understood what his father was getting at, and no doubt Isabelle did, as well. But for the sake of everyone else in the room, he noted, "Once the crown has passed from King Philip, he will have no further legal claim to the throne. He cannot reclaim the crown."

"My father and mother had four children." Isabelle's voice filled with emotion as she spoke. "My oldest brother, Thaddeus, who should have been the heir, disappeared six years ago and was presumed murdered. My brother Alexander is the second child and heir apparent. I am next in line to the throne following Alexander, and my sister, Anastasia, is after me."

Nicolas Grenaldo's deep voice carried clearly in spite of the gentle tone he used. "Regardless of who may technically come before you, Isabelle, you are the only one we know to have escaped the attack. You are the only person who can reclaim the crown on behalf of the royal house of Lydia."

"I can't." Isabelle shook her head. "I can't claim the crown, not while there's still a possibility that my father may be alive."

"You may not have a choice," Nicolas said firmly.

"I may not have the option," Isabelle protested. "I fled the country to save my life. Is it safe for me to return?"

"We can make it safe."

"How?" Levi demanded his father explain. "We don't even know what we're up against. We don't know who our enemies are."

"Perhaps we need to flush them out," Isabelle murmured almost to herself.

"What about the UN?" Samantha Klein asked, stepping out from behind Isabelle's shadow. "Can't they protect Isabelle? Why haven't they done anything to intervene?"

Levi barely had to raise his head to answer. "Did the UN intervene when John F. Kennedy was assassinated? Did the UN step in when the President of Poland and dozens of other Polish leaders were killed in a plane crash? No. Because their governments had rules of succession in place for just such an eventuality. What is the current situation in Lydia?" Levi addressed his father. "Is the military having any trouble keeping the peace?"

Nicolas looked solemn. "Other than the piles of flowers being placed at the gates of the royal palace, little has changed. The military is keeping the peace. Government bodies—the postal service, police, airport authority—are all operating on faith that the situation will be peaceably resolved. But how long they can remain operating in a state of anarchy is anybody's guess."

"I don't believe there is a state of anarchy. Someone is calling the shots," Isabelle insisted. "Someone has committed a crime against my family—and they're still committing it as long as they remain at large."

"We don't know who," Nicolas acknowledged. "Perhaps we should send in a team to investigate Valli, to find out who he's working with and who is behind the attacks." He looked around the room.

The men who had been standing silent for so long now looked down and away. Their response didn't bother Levi. Without Lydian connections he couldn't imagine any of them making inroads—certainly not as quickly as they needed them made. Levi supported his father's plan. "If we can bring evidence before the UN Security Council that an act of aggression has been committed, that the current situation presents a threat to the peace, then the United Nations could be compelled to intervene. All we need is proof. We need someone on the inside. Someone who can get an audience with Valli and the generals."

"I'll go." Princess Isabelle spoke without the slightest hint of hesitation in her voice.

Levi opened his mouth to protest. Only the day before she'd trembled with fear at the thought of facing Valli again. "Isa—"

"My family may be alive somewhere." She cut him off before he could say her name. "If they are, I have no doubt they face grave danger. Every minute the insurgents remain in power increases the odds that my family members may be captured or killed. The only thing I can do to help them is to learn who was behind the attacks and bring that party to justice. We must act quickly. The lives of my parents and siblings are hanging in the balance."

Levi watched the princess with pride and growing affection. He knew her fear of Valli was strong, but love for her family was stronger.

Nicolas Grenaldo nodded solemnly. "You will not go alone. We can assemble a team to provide backup for you. And I will send my son as your coagent."

"Levi and I have learned to work well together."

"I'm sorry." Nicolas cleared his throat. "Not that son. Levi was only marginally successful in bringing you to safety. And he's injured. The boy can hardly stand up on his own.

My son Joe has just returned from another mission. He ca
go with you."

To Levi's surprise, Isabelle stepped closer to him an
placed a gentle hand on his shoulder. "Do you feel up to an
other mission?"

He smiled at her beautiful face in spite of himself. I
he turned down this mission and let Joe take the credit fo
whatever might be accomplished, then Joe would be the nex
Sanctuary president. And Joe would be the one spending tim
with Isabelle.

But then again, maybe Joe was the better man for the job
Joe had more experience. And Joe could stand up on his own
Levi knew that if their mission failed because of his injurie
or lack of experience, he'd never forgive himself. "My great
est concern is for your safety," he began.

"I trust you," she said softly.

Levi swallowed, a sick dread swirling in his stomach. H
had the trust of the princess. But did he deserve that trust
Was he strong enough to keep her safe?

"Fine." His father circled around the table. "I want you
two on the next flight to Lydia. I'll contact Prime Ministe
Emini and let her know you're on your way. We'll take in a
separate team for backup, but I won't tell Emini, Valli or any
of the generals about them. They will be waiting just out o
sight to protect you if need be and to get you out of there i
you get in over your heads. I won't have a repeat of your las
adventure."

Isabelle didn't hesitate but turned to face Nicolas. "Than
you for your thoughtfulness. What's our cover?"

The Sanctuary president smiled. "You're the princess. He'
your bodyguard. Unless your father or older brother step
forward, *you* are the heir to the Lydian throne. And I believe
Lydia's laws stipulate that Parliament controls the corona
tion."

Isabelle appeared to take a moment absorbing the situation. Then she asked, "What about Valli?"

When everyone looked uncertain, one of the men who'd entered with Nicolas spoke up. "Should we request his cooperation? If the reason for your return is to investigate Valli, you'll need to get close to him."

"He's right." Nicolas nodded.

Isabelle still looked hesitant. "But can he be trusted?"

Levi let go of the table and placed a hand on Isabelle's arm, and if he leaned on her somewhat, she didn't seem to mind. "If the whole world knows you're under Valli's care, he'll know better than to hurt you. And if you feel you're in danger again, you won't have to rely on me to get you out of the country this time. We'll have a backup team at the ready. And we'll hold a press conference before you leave the United States. The whole world will know where you are, and they'll be watching."

The trust and determination that simmered in Isabelle's eyes sent Levi's stomach rocking. Or perhaps it was just the effort from standing up. Either way, a sick feeling crept up from his gut. He'd do his best to keep Isabelle safe and return the throne to her family. But would his best be enough?

"Then it's settled." Nicolas nodded with authority. "Isabelle, Samantha will get you everything you need. We can get you back home by the time the sun rises in Lydia."

Levi gave her what he hoped was an encouraging smile, then watched as Isabelle followed Samantha from the room. What had he just agreed to do? They were heading right back into the troubled world they'd worked so hard to escape. And he was in a lot worse shape now than he had been when they'd started out the last time.

"Lord, help us," he prayed quietly as everyone else left the room. "We're going to need a miracle. Possibly several miracles."

EIGHT

Isabelle felt grateful for all of Samantha's help packing. The woman was full of insights into Sanctuary's methods. She also seemed to know a fair bit about Levi.

"I wonder if Levi is up to this mission," Isabelle worried aloud. Although she hoped Nicolas had only been exaggerating, it had seemed as though Levi was hardly strong enough to stand up on his own. He'd certainly leaned heavily on her arm.

Samantha clucked her tongue. "Levi has no choice but to make sure this mission is successful."

"What do you mean?" Isabelle felt grateful for the supplies Sanctuary was providing for her trip. She made a mental note to pay them back when she was restored to her rightful role.

Assuming her family ever regained the throne.

"Levi's father is retiring next year. He'll appoint one of his sons as president after him. Everyone knows he favors Joe, even though Levi is older."

"Joe," Isabelle repeated the name. "That's the son he offered to send with me."

"Joe has more experience with military operations. He's a hero. Levi's just—" Samantha laughed "—a lawyer." She made a face as though the idea of Levi saving anyone was a ridiculous notion. "If I were you, I'd ask to have Joe accompany you, not Levi. I mean, the guy could hardly stand up."